BEV

BEV

Andrea Williams and Matty Rich

Based on a book by Meredith Kopald

A Novel

KAREN HUNTER PUBLISHING   GALLERY BOOKS
New York   London   Toronto   Sydney   New Delhi

Gallery Books
An Imprint of Simon & Schuster, Inc.
1230 Avenue of the Americas
New York, NY 10020

Karen Hunter Publishing
A Division of Suitt-Hunter Enterprises, LLC
P.O. Box 632
South Orange, NJ 07079

First Karen Hunter Publishing/Gallery Books trade paperback edition June 2016

GALLERY BOOKS and colophon are registered trademarks of Simon & Schuster, Inc.

For information about special discounts for bulk purchases, please contact Simon & Schuster Special Sales at 1-866-506-1949 or business@simonandschuster.com.

The Simon & Schuster Speakers Bureau can bring authors to your live event. For more information or to book an event contact the Simon & Schuster Speakers Bureau at 1-866-248-3049 or visit our website at www.simonspeakers.com.

Interior design by Davina Mock-Maniscalco

Manufactured in the United States of America

10 9 8 7 6 5 4 3 2 1

Library of Congress Cataloging-in-Publication Data is available.

ISBN 978-1-4767-9735-9
ISBN 978-1-4767-9736-6 (ebook)

BEV

ONE

"WE'RE GOING TO Mississippi."

Mickey Schwerner's words were blunt and succinct. He raked his right hand along his scruffy beard as he stared boldly into the eyes of David Dunning, his friend since their days studying social work at Cornell, and fellow compatriot in the New York civil rights movement. David returned Mickey's gaze, his handsome, mocha-colored face absent of expression. He was unsure of how to respond to his friend, to this latest in a long line of fearless—if calculated—efforts.

But Bev, never one to hold her tongue, jumped in immediately. "Who is 'we'?"

"Rita and me," Mickey responded, now holding his wife's hand as it rested atop the dingy table situated in the northwest corner of Shelly's Diner. They exchanged a quick glance and then, as if to confirm their resoluteness, turned back to their friends in unison.

Bev pulled a Kent cigarette from her purse, lit it, and took a long draw before asking, "Are you sure?"

Bev hadn't known Mickey and Rita as long as David had, but she had spent the past few years with them, attending meetings and protests to further the cause of low-income, at-risk Negroes in New York. She knew they were wholly committed to the cause, as was she. She'd heard about Mickey successfully integrating Cornell's chapter of the Alpha Epsilon Pi fraternity as an undergrad, and she was there when he and Rita, a schoolteacher, worked to integrate the Gwynn Oak Amusement Park in Maryland. Most recently, Bev had been present to watch the Schwerners in action as they led Manhattan's Lower East Side branch of the Congress of Racial Equality, otherwise known as CORE.

Bev also knew that Mickey had been transfixed by the Birmingham riots just a year prior, as the entire nation sat glued to television sets and newspaper articles that provided eyewitness accounts of the mayhem that ensued when Negro residents took to the streets following a series of bombings targeting Dr. Martin Luther King Jr. and his family.

On May 10, 1963, King had been on hand for the Birmingham Truce Agreement, a proposed compromise among city representatives and local business leaders that called for partial desegregation of public facilities, including retail store fitting rooms and water fountains, as well as economic advancement opportunities for Negro workers. There was also to be a Committee on Racial Problems and Employment formed as a result of the agreement.

But, in typical supremacist fashion, Bull Connor, Birmingham's notorious commissioner of public safety, denounced the so-called truce and threatened to impede its enforcement. Meanwhile, as King and other Negro leaders basked in their apparent victory, KKK leaders from across the South were coordinating a series of attacks, with some believed to have involved officers of the Birmingham Police Department directly.

Neither of the bombs detonated on May 11 — one outside of King's brother's home and another at the Gaston Motel, where King had been staying—were successful in reaching their intended target, or anyone else, for that matter. But that did little to douse the flames of fury that had been rising within the community of oppressed and depressed Negroes for generations.

When the fire finally burst forth, angry Negroes took to the streets of Birmingham, determined to seek their own justice. Some, like the three men who slashed the torso of Officer J. N. Spivey, worked in direct opposition to King's nonviolent credo. It was almost fitting, though, as Birmingham's own response was swift, strong, and equally violent, and included state troopers who beat back protestors while armed with machine guns.

These scenes of unrest were, ultimately, what fertilized the seed of social discontent already taking root in Mickey's heart, feeding it until it became this monster of a thing that demanded more, more, more until finally, Mickey was willing to put his life on the line for the freedom of others.

Bev knew this, but she was still taken aback by this latest declaration. *Mississippi?* The hotbed—both literally and figuratively—of the nation's cruelest bigotry? Where tempers of the racist powers that be rose quicker than sweltering August temperatures? *That* Mississippi?

And what about Rita? she wondered. Sure, there were women who had been involved in the movement, but to voluntarily place his wife of just under two years on the front lines of the civil rights struggle—had Mickey lost his mind?

"Mississippi is where we need to be," Mickey said. "The work we're doing here in New York is great, but in the Deep South, we're not talking about whether Negroes can buy a home in a certain part of town. We're talking about basic human rights." He paused for a beat, then lowered his voice for effect. "Did you know that in Mississippi, only six percent of the eligible Negro population is registered to vote? Those people have been stripped of their ability to control their futures and the future of their family."

Mickey then turned to Bev, as if somehow surmising her thoughts and answering them directly. His brown eyes sparkled with excitement as he spoke. "Rita and I have discussed this extensively," he said, gripping her hand even tighter now. "We are not at all naive to the grave danger, but we also refuse to sit idle while innocent people are subjected to such cruelty. We just can't. Rita and I are taking this step together."

Bev took another draw of her cigarette, feeling a sense of pride and admiration welling within her, displacing the worry and concern that had tried to take root. Bev had spent her entire career—her entire life, really—in a painstaking effort to level the playing field for all people, regardless of race or gender. And here she was, sitting across from two people who, in bearing the same white skin as she, may not have had a direct, personal link to the civil rights movement, but who were as passionate and steadfast as if their own ancestors had once been enslaved.

Certainly, with Mickey and Rita having only been married for a couple of years, it seemed more appropriate for them to be honeymooning in some tropical locale than venturing off into the dark underbelly of American racism. But as Mickey emphasized the word "together," Bev understood that this move was, in fact, a symbol of their love and dedication to their marriage vows and to each other, to supporting that which most compelled them. She could only hope that she would one day have a husband whose innermost desires aligned so closely with her own.

While David remained silent, poking solemnly at his chicken salad, Bev pressed on. "So what will you be doing, exactly?"

"Well," said Rita, "CORE is establishing a community center in Meridian, Mississippi, that will provide many of the basic services that the state and local authorities refuse to provide for Negroes. We'll be able to help the adults understand their rights as citizens, while also teaching the children subjects that they'd never have access to in public schools.

"It's amazing, really, this idea that we'll be able to have a direct impact on these people, not just right now, but for generations to come," she added, her voice soft and demure but just as firm as her husband's. "Access to quality education has the ability to change the course of a person's life more completely and effectively than any other variable."

Bev smiled as she reached across the table with both arms, placing her hands on top of the couple's. "Well, I wish you all the best of luck and safe travels. The movement needs boldly courageous people, and it may very well take people like you, willing to leave the comfort of the North, to finally effect real change." Then, speaking directly to Rita, she added, "I would do the same."

Rita smiled back at Bev, her petite face overwhelmed by an expression as genuine as the burning hatred they would soon encounter. "Thank you, Bev. That means a lot. We leave on the fifteenth, but I promise to stay in touch."

As a busboy arrived to clear the dishes from the table, Bev, Mickey, and Rita stood to pull on their overcoats and scarves, bracing themselves for the bitter January cold.

Finally, David, still seated, broke his silence. "Hey, Mickey. What about Johnson?" he asked, referring to President Lyndon B. Johnson, who had recently taken office following the assassination of JFK in November.

"What about him?"

"You know, the civil rights legislation that Kennedy proposed last summer. After that mess in Birmingham, Johnson's promising to push it through Congress." David stood from the rickety table and shoved his hands into his coat pockets while he waited for Mickey's response.

"That's great, man. We want that to happen," Mickey said, not deterred. "But in the meantime, we are the hands and feet of the movement. We must demand change *now*. Not *when* or *if* Johnson gets around to passing some bill."

"But what if you don't make it back?" Silence washed over the friends as all eyes turned toward Mickey. And though David's question wasn't enough to completely deflate the lifting excitement that Mickey still registered on his face, it accurately addressed the concern that, until that point, had gone unuttered.

"Then I don't make it back," Mickey said, stoic as ever. "I have a very real, emotional need to offer my services in the South, and I plan on working until the end of my life toward a just, equal society. If the end comes sooner than later, so be it."

The city streets were still littered with remnants of the prior day's New Year's celebrations, and as they stepped out onto the sidewalk in front of Shelly's, Bev and David found themselves sidestepping plastic kazoos and party hats emblazoned with "1964."

"You wanna take a cab?" David asked, interrupting Bev's thoughts, the same thoughts she'd had in the diner, thoughts that had been swimming around in her head ever since Mickey first made public his decision to journey below the Mason-Dixon Line.

"No, I think I'd rather walk."

Bev's house at 910 West End Avenue wasn't far from Shelly's—hence Bev's infatuation with the restaurant's chicken soup with egg noodles—but she wasn't quite ready to go home yet. She had some things she needed to discuss with David, and a taxi ride would have landed her at her doorstep in less than five minutes.

Professionally, Bev was adept at the art of effective communication. She had recently been promoted at Hillside Hospital, from a staff social worker to a supervisor managing a team of more than ten varying personalities and dispositions. And she was often called on to put out various fires in the field. Just a few weeks prior, she received a call from an Episcopalian priest who had volunteered to sponsor a tutoring program for at-risk children. Unfortunately, when he learned that those at-risk children were primarily Puerto Rican and Negro, and that they would have to actually come to his church to be tutored, he wasn't so sold on the program. *"Those* people," he'd explained to Bev, "can't be trusted. They come from families and homes where sin and violence is commonplace."

And Bev, in considering the most practical, reasonable approach to combat the priest's argument, appealed to his religious sensibilities. "Father," she'd said, "what happened to faith, hope, and charity?"

His reply was equally practical. "They are the cornerstone of what we do here, but I have a faithful congregation I must consider, and I just can't risk bringing those children here."

"So have you been to their homes and actually met their families to see if your presumptions about their home lives are actually valid?" Bev asked.

The priest hemmed and hawed a bit before answering. "To be honest, Miss Luther, I really haven't had the time. I've been busy with administrative duties, and I trust my staff to advise me correctly when it comes to matters such as these."

"I see," said Bev, in the most calculated way. "Well, Father, in that case, it's a shame that the tutoring must stop."

"Why so?"

"It is quite unfortunate—but very realistic—to consider that, without the educational advantage your tutoring program could provide, these children may be forced to resort to illegal methods of survival as they navigate through life. Methods that could potentially impact this very neighborhood where your church now sits."

The priest changed his mind about shuttering the program, and even Bev's boss was surprised by the rapid turnaround. But while talking was one of the few things that Bev knew she did well, here, with David, she had to choose her words carefully.

"Do you think Mickey's making a mistake?" she asked, looking up into David's face. With Bev standing at just five feet two, and David towering almost a full foot above her, Bev had to strain to make out any reaction on his face as he continued to silently place one foot in front of the other.

"Why do you ask that?" he said, slowing his pace just slightly.

"I don't know. At Shelly's, it just seemed like, like . . . like you weren't excited for them."

"Excited for them? What do you mean excited? Are *you* excited for them?" David stopped walking and turned to face Bev directly, his long arms folded across his chest.

"Actually, I am, yes," Bev replied. "I can really see the great potential in the work they're going to do. Don't you?"

Bev was surprised when she saw a smile spreading across David's handsome face, even more so when she heard him laughing. "What's so funny?" she asked, visibly irritated.

"You know, it's really *not* funny," said David, now serious. "Y'all just don't have a clue."

"What's that supposed to mean?"

"Give me a break, Bev. I grew up in Wilkinson County, Mississippi, in a tiny town called Centreville. You know that."

"Yes, I do know that. But I don't understand what that has to do with Mickey and Rita. I would think you'd be happy that they would care enough about what's happening in your home state, so close to where you grew up, to try and make a difference."

"That's just the thing, Bev. I've lived that life. Seen it with my own two eyes. Those good ol' boys down there ain't playing games. They don't care nothin' about Martin Luther King, so you know they ain't gon' care about two uppity nigger lovers from New York."

"But Mickey said they've considered the danger—"

"How can they consider the danger when they don't even know what they don't know?" David's face was dark now, and the corners of his eyes were welling with tears.

"Have you ever seen a man hanging from a tree?" he said. "I'm not talking about a newspaper photo, or some TV news program. I'm talking about driving to the grocery store to pick up some flour and a couple of potatoes and passing right by a man dangling from an oak tree, no doubt strung up for some trivial offense like not stepping off the sidewalk to make way for a five-year-old white girl."

Bev didn't know how to respond. She'd heard David speak of his past before, but never with so much intensity. She fumbled in her purse for a cigarette while he kept talking.

"I've seen gangs of a dozen white men beat a Negro boy in the middle of town in broad daylight, with folks walking right by and not saying a word. And if you think you're just gon' call the police, forget about it. Half the time, they're the ones organizing the attacks."

"But, David," Bev started, "we know the danger is very real. Even if Mickey hasn't seen the danger for himself, I'm sure his imagination has provided him with plenty of material. So what then? Is he supposed to ignore his call to fight? And what about the people he would be turning his back on? What about them?"

Bev and David finished the walk to Bev's house in silence, twin clouds of smoke gathering and then disappearing in front of their faces as they breathed in the twenty-degree air.

Once at her stoop, Bev took a hard look at this man who had become her best friend, with whom she'd shared so much of her life. She completely understood his position regarding Mickey and Rita's decision, and it pained her to see that he himself was torn. How do you choose between justice and personal safety? Life and freedom for others or that for yourself?

"I'm sorry if I upset you," said Bev.

"When my dad packed up our family to move to New York, my brothers were too young to understand the significance of those thousand miles he was placing between us and our past," David responded. "So now, they don't understand why Dad doesn't want to go to sit-ins or protests or watch news updates on the movement. But not me. I understood then, and I really understand now."

Bev listened intently while David spoke, though she still wasn't completely convinced by his point of view. Granted, she had never seen the things he had seen, and neither had Mickey or Rita. But it also made sense to her that their friends wanted to take their involvement to the next level, to do the work that mattered in the place where it mattered most. From that perspective, then, the inherent risks, grave as they were, seemed more like a technical nuisance than a logical deterrent.

"So you would never consider going?" Bev asked, leaning her small frame against her front door.

David paused before answering. "When you are a Negro man in Mississippi, there is a large part of your existence that is dedicated to simply *surviving*. Planning for a future, sending your kids to college, those things aren't even a factor when all of your energies must be focused on waking up to see tomorrow."

He cleared his throat, then added, "My father changed that for our family. He sacrificed so no other Dunning man would have to fear for his life if he was stranded without gas on a country road after dark. He ensured that the women in our family could be more than cooks and maids. To be honest, I just can't see myself voluntarily returning to a place that has meant nothing but death and darkness for my family."

Bev felt as if the weight of David's words were crushing her heart. "Wow, David," she said. "I didn't know you felt that way. There's not really much I can say to that." She shifted from one foot to the other. "But what about Mickey and Rita? They haven't shared your experiences, so why are you so against them helping the people who are in the same position you were years ago, but who lack the resources or will to simply pack up and move north?"

David's voice grew soft, so soft that Bev could hardly hear him above the sound of the train in the distance. "I understand Mickey and Rita's motives; really I do," he said. "But I'm scared for them. To southerners, being so cursed to have black skin is bad enough. But to be blessed with white skin and make the *choice* to join forces with the Negroes, thus threatening the only way of life those evil segregationists have ever known? The way of life they've worked so hard to maintain? That is completely reprehensible—far worse than the poor soul who was born Negro through no cause of his own.

"So as far as Mickey and Rita are concerned," David continued, "I can't lie. I'm scared, and I don't know if I'll see my friends alive again."

It was at that moment that Bev decided against divulging the secret desire that had been growing in her own heart from the moment they stepped out of Shelly's—that she, too, wanted to head south.

TWO

Six months later . . .

DR. KLEINFELD'S OFFICE was in an abandoned dry cleaner facility just a mile and a half from Hillside Hospital. The building was so nondescript, in fact, that Bev would have likely walked right past it if she hadn't been visiting the psychiatrist twice weekly for more than eighteen months.

Bev knew that some people thought it strange that a clinical social worker saw a therapist regularly, but she believed so much in the benefit of working through personal struggles with someone else that she wanted to experience it for herself. In fact, she could find no logical reason why she *shouldn't* seek therapy. To her, the thought of not doing so was as arcane as that of a butcher who didn't eat meat.

It wasn't that Bev was psychotic or out of her mind; she simply valued the professional opinion of someone who wasn't as deeply vested in her life as she was—someone who could give her the objective perspective that she often lacked. And while her conversations with Dr. Kleinfeld danced to all corners of her life—including her career, social life, and romantic involvements (or lack thereof)—most sessions inevitably snaked their way around the topic of her mother.

"Hey there, Bev!"

As soon as she pulled on the glass door with the fading black and red sign that read "OPEN," Bev was greeted by Nancy. Nancy was a striking woman in her fifties who had been working as Dr. Kleinfeld's secretary since she moved to New York from Cincinnati following the death of her husband five years prior. If Bev didn't know any better, she'd think Nancy's sunny disposition was a direct result of the almost constant time she spent with the doctor.

"Hi, Nancy. You look really nice today." Bev eyed the emerald-colored shift that almost perfectly matched Nancy's eyes. It was certainly beautiful and it fit all of her curves just so, but it was a bit too much for this sticky Tuesday in the middle of another sweltering New York summer. Bev smoothed the wrinkles in her long linen skirt before leaning casually on the front counter. She sometimes resented the fact that people didn't take her seriously after looking over her slight build and mousy features, but she would much rather let her convictions prove her worth before resorting—like Nancy—to her feminine wiles.

"Thanks, honey!" Nancy said, beaming at the compliment while she did a little shimmy. "I picked this little thing up last Friday after work, and I just can't believe how comfortable it is. Dr. K. even said it brings out the green in my eyes."

"Well, I can vouch for that; it certainly does," Bev said, smiling. "Is he ready for me yet? I only have about thirty minutes today, so I'd like to get started."

"Oh, yes, of course. You just wait right there and let me check on him for you." Nancy shimmied past the artificial partition that divided the front reception area and the back of the building where Dr. Kleinfeld met with his patients. After a couple of minutes of muted conversation and soft giggles, Nancy re-emerged and announced that Bev could head back.

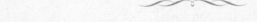

"It's good to see you, Beverly," Dr. Kleinfeld started. "You haven't been in much since your promotion at work, so tell me, how are things?"

"It's great, really, Dr. K. It's a lot of responsibility, and I'm not working directly with the kids as much anymore, but I love it. My colleagues value my contributions, and that's all I could ask for." Bev settled back into the red and yellow plaid overstuffed chair that sat across from Dr. K.'s desk and searched for a cigarette inside her purse. Satisfied after locating one, she asked for a light.

"I'm glad to hear that. Now, tell me again, what types of children do you treat at Hillside?" Dr. K. reached across his desk with a lighter.

"Well, most of the kids are referred by a cry for help."

"And what is that, exactly?"

"Well, as an example, we recently received a teenage boy, probably around fifteen years old, who went into the garage at his parents' house, found a can of paint and a paintbrush, and painted himself red. We consider that a cry for help."

"I would say so," said Dr. K., with the same solemn expression that seemed permanently affixed to his face. "So do you think you are still having as great an impact now that you're on the administrative side, working with the other staffers? Do you miss working with the patients?"

Bev paused. She hadn't considered that maybe she *was* feeling a bit discontented with her work. She wondered whether that was at the root of her willingness to look for other outlets to pursue—even dangerous ones.

"I believe so," she said finally, thinking out loud. "But, you know, maybe it's kind of good this way because it gives me a chance to really become more active in civil rights work."

"Oh? And what does that mean—more active?"

"Well, you know I've been working with local organizations . . . but I've been thinking about expanding my reach some . . ." Bev was tentative, mostly because after David's reaction, she wasn't sure whether her bright idea was so smart after all. "I've been thinking about doing some work in the South, where people are most in need."

Dr. K. peered at Bev above his tortoise-rimmed bifocals and took a long pause. "Have you thought that through, Beverly? Really?"

"Yes, I have . . ." She hesitated. "Well, just a little, actually."

"The work in Mississippi and Alabama is certainly important, Beverly, but it's also very dangerous. I know you understand that."

"I do. And I'm willing to take the risk. I have two friends from New York who are in Mississippi right now, working to register voters and establish a community center in Meridian. They left in January, and I've received several letters detailing their experience and how humbled and honored they are to have the opportunity to do what they're doing."

"And your friends, they've remained safe?" Dr. K. asked, still skeptical.

"Well, of course they've received some death threats, and local bigots have been working overtime to intimidate them to the point of their retreat. But they are fully vested, Doctor. And where is the reward—for themselves and the Negro people of Mississippi—without the risk?"

"It does seem as though you've given it some thought. But what does your mother think about this?"

There it was, that ever-present topic of conversation. "I haven't talked to her about it, actually," Bev said, sighing heavily while tapping out her cigarette butt in the marble ashtray on Dr. K.'s desk.

"Why not?"

"For starters, we're still arguing about me getting a car."

~~~~~

It was December 1953 when Bev was visiting her mom and sister at home in California during her holiday break from the University of Chicago. She had arranged a ride back to school with a fellow student whose name she found on a bulletin board where individuals offered and accepted rides. Bev met Jim Anderson on New Year's Day 1954, when he came to pick her up. He was a freshman at the University of Chicago, a tall, skinny, eighteen-year-old blond kid with a bad case of acne that made him look even younger. Jim was driving a Chevrolet convertible, and he and Bev planned to pick up Highway 66 in Bakersfield and then drive all the way to Chicago—a distance of some two thousand miles—taking turns driving.

On the first day, they got as far as Bakersfield and then drove through the desert at night, stopping for breakfast the next morning in Needles, Arizona. From Needles to Flagstaff, the road climbs to seven thousand feet and crosses a pass thick with pine trees. There was snow on the road, slowing them down, but from Flagstaff, Bev and Jim went on without stopping through the second night, crossing the border from Arizona into New Mexico. It was bitter cold (on Sunday, January 3, the high in Albuquerque was just thirty-one degrees), and in the convertible the heater was on full blast. Bev and Jim had just covered more than a thousand miles in forty-eight hours without a break.

They had planned on stopping in Albuquerque for breakfast and a rest, but eighteen miles out, around seven in the morning, Bev fell asleep at the wheel. The car turned over three times, and she was thrown headfirst through the windshield, landing facedown on the frozen ground. A truck driver stopped and sent motorists to call an ambulance while he covered her with blankets and built a fire to keep her warm.

Bev regained consciousness in the emergency room of Presbyterian Hospital. She was badly bruised with facial cuts, but her most severe injury was a fractured skull: shattered bone had embedded in her brain. By extraordinary luck, Dr. Leroy J. Miller was passing through the emergency room when Beverly was brought in. It was a coincidence that most certainly saved her life, since in 1954, Dr. Miller was the only neurosurgeon in New Mexico.

In the emergency room, Dr. Miller examined Bev and arranged an immediate operation to remove the bits of bone and to close the wound. Removal of the bone left the brain vulnerable, though, so a second operation would have to be performed at a later date. So much damage had been done that when Bev emerged from the operating room, she had a deep depression on the right side of her forehead, just above her eyebrow. It was disfiguring, but it was also the only visible evidence of the injury. There was no scar, because Dr. Miller had been able to work through the top of Bev's skull, above the hairline, pulling the skin of her forehead down to expose the brain. Her hair grew back quickly, and the incision at her hairline was never visible.

Because Bev was never in a coma and was actually conscious in the emergency room, Dr. Miller was able to explain the procedure to her. Bev insisted on calling home to tell her mother. She was typically calm, while her mother, of course, was not. The next day, Bev's mother took the train to Albuquerque and stayed with Bev until her release from the hospital twenty-seven days later. Jim, badly bruised but not seriously hurt, spent several days in the hospital, and then returned to Chicago by bus.

More than ten years had passed since the accident, but Bev's mother made it painfully clear that she still didn't want her daughter driving. And in an effort to somewhat appease her mother—even from more than three thousand miles away—Bev had refrained from buying a car. So every morning she woke up extra early to take the train from her home to Hillside Hospital in Queens.

"You can understand her position, can't you?" Dr. K. asked.

"Not really," Bev snapped back. "I *am* an adult."

"Yes, yes, you are. But you are also her child, her youngest child. Perhaps when you have a child, you will more easily see things from her point of view."

Bev dipped her head so that Dr. K. couldn't see the pain that washed across her face. It didn't work.

"What's wrong? Did I say something offensive?" Dr. K. asked.

"It's nothing. I'm fine." Bev grabbed for another cigarette.

"Beverly, you are here to talk, so please tell me what concerns you."

Bev lit the end of her cigarette and inhaled deeply before answering. "I just want more, Dr. K. I'm very happy with my career, and I love the fact that I can help change lives on a daily basis, but it's not enough. I want a family."

"Is there a specific source of your dissatisfaction?"

"No, I don't think so. I mean, it's always been my desire to have children and a husband I'm madly in love with." Bev paused, then added, "I wouldn't be honest, though, if I didn't admit that seeing my friends in serious relationships didn't cause me to envy them just a bit. And my sister, Meredith, who's only a year older than me, has a husband and *three* kids already."

"Are you actively trying to meet men?" Dr. K. asked. "What kinds of social activities are you participating in?"

"None, really," Bev said pitifully. "I don't have time, with work and the movement . . ."

"Well, what about your friend David? You two seem to spend a lot of time together, and I've only heard you say positive things about him. Is he someone you could be interested in pursuing a relationship with?"

Bev was shocked by Dr. K.'s suggestion. "No! Of course not! I mean, we're just friends. Good friends . . ."

"Okay, Beverly, I understand. I only meant that, if you're saying you're having a hard time meeting people, you may want to look to those closest to you already."

"That makes sense, Dr. K. But not David. I just don't understand why I can't find the right guy—the perfect guy. I want what Meredith has."

Dr. K. nodded. "Of course, but you do have a very noble career and, by your own admission, you are committed to being an active participant in the civil rights movement, which is quite noble as well. Your sister's in Vietnam now, right?"

"Um-hmm." Bev took another draw on her cigarette. "Meredith's husband works for the Agency for International Development, and they're in Vietnam while he finishes a two-year tour of duty. But I don't see how that's relevant—"

"Would you be willing to make that kind of sacrifice?" Dr. K. asked, cutting Bev off. "Could you sacrifice the work you're doing, the work you're most passionate about, to follow your husband's dreams? Would *that* be enough for you?"

"Absolutely!" Bev shouted without a moment's hesitation. "If I knew, for sure, that he was wholeheartedly committed to me, to his family, I would most certainly follow him wherever he wanted to go."

"And you're sure about that?"

"Yes, sir, I am."

By the time Beverly made it home, it was well past six o'clock, and she was exhausted and starving. Her session with Dr. K. had lasted more than an hour, not the thirty minutes she had planned for. She felt it had been productive, though, so she didn't mind that she had to head back to her office to wade through a mountain of paperwork before she could leave for the day.

She wasn't as productive when she got back to work, though, because her mind kept drifting back to Dr. K.'s questions about her relationship with David. Truthfully, things had been a bit strained since their dinner with Mickey and Rita in January. They were still close and saw each other at least once a week, but Bev found herself a bit guarded, intentionally avoiding topics that she thought could incite more anger or sadness or whatever he had been feeling that New Year's night. And now, as she stood in her kitchen, putting on a pot of coffee, she gave the conversation even more thought.

Was it possible that she could have deeper feelings for David? Was David boyfriend material? Could she see herself in a long-term relationship with him?

As she thought about being more than friends with David, she was unable to come up with any reasons why she shouldn't consider it. By all practical measures, David was a catch. He was tall and strikingly handsome, with dark, searching eyes and lips that looked pillow soft. And he was bright and ambitious and hardworking in a way that reminded her of her father. Best of all, they already knew each other so well, so there wouldn't be any of that awkward getting-to-know-you phase or a strained first date. But there was one question that she couldn't shake from her head.

Had David ever thought of her romantically?

To that last question, Bev tried searching the furthest corners of her mind for any past interactions that may have conveyed, even in the most subtle sense, that David had romantic feelings for her. She was coming up short. David was kind and caring, and they often shared a warm embrace, but Bev felt she would be exaggerating greatly if she assumed that he had ever had any romantic inclinations toward her.

But would it matter if he didn't share her feelings? Would that change how she felt about him?

Bev shook her head violently, as if to physically discharge

the offending thoughts from her mind. David was perfect husband material, sure, but Bev wasn't certain that he was meant to be *her* husband.

Just as she was rummaging through the refrigerator, looking for the leftover chicken fried rice from Mama Po's that she'd had the night before, Marianne popped into the kitchen.

"How was Dr. K.?" she asked.

"Good," said Bev. "Stayed a little longer than I intended, but it was worth it."

"He's wonderful, isn't he? I'm scheduled to see him tomorrow, and I can't wait to talk to him about the new guy I've been seeing."

Bev ignored her roommate and tried to forget the fact that she'd actually referred Marianne to her own private therapist. Bev had tried to keep Dr. K. to herself, telling Marianne that she was the most well-adjusted person she knew, so she certainly didn't need therapy, but Marianne had persisted like a spoiled child. Like Bev's other roommates, Elaine and Barbara, Marianne was in social work. Bev knew she had the same intense need for an objective sounding board for her deepest concerns, so she'd finally relented and passed along Dr. Kleinfeld's phone number. But that didn't mean she wanted to hear about Marianne's sessions with him.

"Have you seen my Chinese food from last night?" Bev asked.

"What Chinese food?"

"Never mind." Bev opted instead for a turkey sandwich on rye with lettuce and tomato. She could hear the phone ringing from the living room while she was making her dinner, and she was smearing on the last of the Miracle Whip when Marianne shouted her name to tell her it was for her. Bev left her sandwich on the counter and grabbed a cigarette before settling in on the couch next to the phone table.

"Hello?" No response. "Hello?" Bev said again, as she pressed her ear to the phone, but she could hear little more than someone's ragged breathing on the other end. Assuming the caller had the wrong number, Bev was just about to hang up when she finally heard a voice.

"Bev. It's Rita."

"Rita! Hi! How are you?" Bev asked the question, but she immediately knew the answer, as Rita's soft, strained voice told her clearly that all was not well.

"I'm . . . I'm okay," Rita said, almost whispering. "But I'm calling . . . I'm calling . . ."

"What's the matter, Rita?" Bev was trying to piece together Rita's words, but she was having a hard time and growing more anxious and concerned by the second.

"It's Mickey, Bev. They can't find him."

Now Bev was really confused. "Who is 'they,' Rita? And what do you mean they can't find him?"

"They, the authorities, they don't know where he is. I mean, he's in Mississippi, but that's all we know. He's been missing since the Sunday before last."

Bev glanced up at the calendar on the wall. It was June 30 and two Sundays prior was the twenty-first. Nine days and Rita hadn't heard from her husband. She had no idea where he was or whether he was safe. Bev stopped herself from thinking the worst.

"What have the police told you?" she asked.

In between steady tears and some full-out sobs, Rita managed to relay the bits of information that she knew regarding Mickey's last known whereabouts. She told Bev that while she and Mickey had been working in Mississippi, they were summoned to Ohio to take part in a special training for college students who were going to be taking buses to Mississippi to help register Negroes to vote. They were happy to do it, Rita said, but they were also concerned about the people they were leaving behind.

Sure enough, after they had been in Ohio a couple of weeks, they got word that Mt. Zion United Methodist Church in Philadelphia, Mississippi, where they had been doing some organizing, was burned to the ground. Naturally, Mickey wanted to go back and check on the church and community members, and Rita encouraged him to. "He had to go back and see those people," Rita said. "You don't abandon people who have put themselves at risk."

On Saturday, June 20, Mickey left Ohio along with Andrew Goodman, another white civil rights worker, and J. E. Chaney, a Negro man from Mississippi, and headed to Meridian in a blue station wagon. They arrived in Meridian safely, and on Sunday they drove to Philadelphia to see the church. That evening, Rita received the phone call that had turned her world upside down.

"I'm so sorry," Bev said, now fighting back her own tears. "But there's still hope. He's missing, but he's not dead. There's still hope. Don't worry."

There was another long silence on the line, then Rita blew her nose. "You're right, Bev. You're right. Please just don't tell David yet, okay? I don't want him to worry."

Bev declined to mention that David had been worried long before they ever even crossed over the New York state line back in January. "I won't," she promised. "And please let me know as soon as you hear something."

"Sure, Bev. Thanks for talking. I'll be in touch soon."

Bev hung up the phone and sat in the quiet for a minute, replaying every horrific detail of the conversation she'd just had with Rita. Then she lit the cigarette that was still clutched in her left hand, walked slowly to the kitchen, and threw her sandwich in the trash before heading to bed.

THREE

ACCORDING TO REPORTS, Mickey, Andrew, and JE had been arrested after leaving Meridian on June 21. Deputy Sheriff Cecil Price pulled over the blue station wagon on an alleged traffic violation and took the three passengers to the Neshoba County jail. They were finally released—in the middle of the night—but there was no sweet freedom, as Mickey and his friends were soon stopped on a rural road by two carloads of Ku Klux Klan members.

It was part of a master plan, apparently, one that was devised by Klan Imperial Wizard Sam Bowers, who had ordered Mickey's death back in May. "Goatee," as Mickey was known to Klan members in and around Meridian, was the most hated of all civil rights workers in the area. His crimes? Organizing a boycott of a local general store that sold mostly to Negroes until it hired its first black employee, and encouraging the countless disenfranchised citizens to register to vote.

Mickey was no doubt aware of the bounty on his head, but that never deterred him from his efforts. "It's the decisive battle-ground," he'd said of the racially charged Magnolia State. "No-where in the world is the idea of white supremacy more firmly entrenched, or more cancerous, than in Mississippi." Mickey's trip to Oxford, Ohio, to train more volunteers may have derailed the Klan's plans momentarily, but they were revived as soon as he rode back into town.

After going undiscovered for forty-four days, Mickey's twenty-four-year-old body, along with Chaney's and Goodman's, was found in an earthen dam. Mickey and Goodman had been shot to death, as had Chaney, but he only after being chain-whipped.

In the days leading up to the discovery of Mickey's body and the ones that followed, Rita kept in touch with Bev as promised. Afterward, she talked little of her husband's tragic fate, instead focusing on the work that still needed to be done and of the dark Mississippi culture that bred the men who committed such a heinous crime.

But Bev didn't need Rita for updates. The story of the three missing civil rights workers had transfixed the nation and mo-nopolized just about every newspaper front page and evening television news report.

"Should we have tea or lemonade?" Bev asked David, as she made her way around David's tiny kitchen to the refrigerator.

"I really don't think it matters."

David was putting the final touches on a roasted chicken with carrots, onions, and potatoes, the cooking of which had elevated the temperature inside his tiny, six-hundred-square-foot apartment to almost match the ninety-eight-degree weather outside. Meanwhile, Bev was frosting a three-layer coconut cream cake using a recipe she'd gotten from her roommate Elaine. The details of their impromptu dinner seemed insignificant at best, especially considering that the newly widowed Rita was their guest of honor, but Bev and David wanted her to have a well-cooked meal, even as everything else around her was falling apart.

"Rita! It's so good to see you."

Bev could hear David's deep voice greeting their friend, and she realized that she had been so focused on her dessert that she hadn't even heard the knock on the door. She'd grabbed three plates from the cabinet above the sink and turned to put them on the table when she saw Rita standing in the kitchen's entryway, pale and slight, with her dark hair in an unkempt bun at the nape of her neck, and a small smile attempting to creep its way across her otherwise broken face.

"Oh, Rita!" Bev cried, hardly masking her emotion. "I'm so,

so sorry . . . Please sit . . . How was your trip? What can I get you?" Bev was babbling, one barely comprehensible sentence running after another, until Rita cut her off.

"I'm fine, Bev. Really," Rita said.

"I-I don't know what to say," Bev stammered. "I just can't imagine . . ."

"You don't have to say anything," answered Rita. "And it's still hard for me to imagine that my husband is gone forever, too. But I don't want to spend the evening feeling sad about that. Mickey fought for what he believed in, and for that I am immensely proud. Let's just enjoy this dinner together. That's what Mickey would want."

Bev and David looked at each other before silently acquiescing.

"Fine," David said as he carried the platter of chicken to the table. "So what can we help you with? Have all of the arrangements been made?"

"Yes. The memorial service will be on August ninth at the Community Church on East Thirty-Fifth Street. I expect you both will be there?"

"Absolutely!" said Bev. "And you're sure there's nothing we can do? We loved Mickey so much and are so devastated by the news . . . We just want to help any way we can."

"Then continue doing what you've been doing," said Rita. "Your work within the movement is more important than ever now. It is unfortunate that it took the deaths of two white men for people to understand the horrific behavior against innocent people that goes unabated in the South, but people are paying attention now."

Rita pulled a small embroidered handkerchief from the front pocket of her pants and dabbed the corners of her eyes. "So you must keep working," she continued. "Keep pushing, keep challenging. Mickey's death cannot be for nothing."

"That's a good point, Rita," said Bev. "You know, if it wasn't for Mickey and Andrew being in that car, JE's family probably would have never known what happened to him. He would have just been another Negro, kidnapped in the middle of the night to never be heard from again."

"I have been watching the news every night," Bev continued, now standing, hands waving wildly as she spoke, "and it's amazing how much the media and authorities have gotten behind this case. They launched an FBI investigation, for Pete's sake! When does that ever happen for a poor Negro from Meridian?"

"Exactly," Rita said, as she sat up a little straighter in her chair. "That's exactly what I mean."

"I mean, in that case, maybe it's a good thing they were killed!"

The room fell silent as the three friends took in the gravity of Bev's words.

"Have you lost your mind?!" David interjected. "I'm not

going to listen to either of you talk about the 'good' that can come from someone dying. I was raised in Mississippi, and obviously, ain't a whole lot changed since I was a boy. Sadly, I knew this could happen."

David stood and turned to face Rita. "No disrespect, Rita, but Mickey was one of my best friends. To me, there's no benefit in me knowing that I'll never see him or speak to him again. That's just my opinion." He bent over and kissed Rita's cheek. "If you'll excuse me, I need to step out for a minute."

"I'm really sorry," Bev said to Rita, once the front door had closed and the two women heard David's heavy steps disappear down the hallway. Her voice was gentler now, as she could see that Rita's eyes were once again glistening with tears. "I hope I didn't offend you, but Mickey's death may have been the catalyst that this movement needed. President Johnson had to force J. Edgar Hoover to open an investigation, but he did. In the process, the bodies of *eight* other Negro men who had been previously missing were discovered. The Civil Rights Act was finally passed. And Walter Cronkite said that this case, those disappearances, were 'the focus of the whole country's concern.'

"We have an opportunity now that this country's never seen," Bev continued. "From now on, the blinding racism that blankets states like Mississippi and Alabama won't just be the South's problem. We will air their dirty laundry for the whole nation and the whole world to see."

Rita nodded in agreement. "It's fine, Bev. I completely un-derstand how you feel." Then she paused. When she spoke again, her words were heavy, beleaguered. "But I also under-stand David. This thing, this movement . . . it's a lot. It takes a whole-life sacrifice and commitment that not many people can make. My husband did, and he did it with a bravery and coura-geousness that amazed me every single day. But I don't know that I can continue without him."

"What do you mean?" Bev's confusion was visible on her face.

"I am heading to the Democratic National Convention at the end of the month," Rita said. "I assisted in the formation of the new Mississippi Freedom Democratic Party, which is com-prised of both Negro and white members. We will have dele-gates at the convention to challenge the authority of the all-white Mississippi Democratic Party, which, of course, has only been able to exist because of the suppression of the Negro vote. Because of this—the fact that the Mississippi Democratic Party delegates were elected in an illegal, segregated vote—we will be arguing for our right to participate in the convention.

"So I will be in Atlantic City August twenty-fourth to the twenty-seventh," Rita added, "but I don't know what I will do after that. Everything has just taken a lot out of me, and I may need a break. I'm thinking about going to law school."

"Law school?!" Bev couldn't hide her surprise. "But what

about your work in Mississippi? You said there's still so much to be done. What about the freedom school and the community center? Who will continue in your place?"

"Bev, my friend, my replacement is the least of my concerns," said Rita. "I met so many young, eager men and women in Ohio this summer who will gladly take over where Mickey and I left off. If I can be sure of any one thing, it's that the movement has a very bright future. I am simply passing the baton."

Bev remembered seeing the summer's news broadcasts from Western College in Oxford, Ohio, where hundreds of bright-eyed, mostly white coeds were gathered to train for the Mississippi Summer Project. Led by members of the Student Nonviolent Coordinating Committee (SNCC) and CORE, the volunteers were briefed in all things Mississippi before embarking on what would be the most rewarding, yet harrowing, journey of their short lives.

They learned the ins and outs of Mississippi's rural geography—particularly what roads were safe to take and which ones weren't, especially after dark. They engaged in role-play, taking turns submitting to the vile, segregationist language and threats that would be hurled at them daily in Mississippi. They learned how to save their lives—how to take a beating and absorb blows in body parts that could withstand the force of pummeling fists and feet.

And they saw, up close and in person, the battle wounds of those who had already braved the savagery of the Ku Klux Klan and other angry white men whose idea of fun was counting the seconds it took for an expertly tied noose to strangle the life from an innocent Negro.

Reporter after reporter shoved microphones in the faces of the would-be volunteers, who hailed mostly from affluent homes on the East Coast. "Are you scared?" the journalists wanted to know. And with youthful naïveté and exuberance most certainly at play, the kids from New York and Maine, Washington, DC and Connecticut answered no every time. While sitting on the couch in the safety of her living room, legs folded under her and casually smoking a cigarette, Bev had marveled at their fearlessness and wondered whether that kind of courage lay within her.

"Well then, Rita," said Bev, bringing her thoughts back to David's kitchen and the uneaten cake with its ivory frosting slowly melting in the stifling heat, "pass the baton if you must. I will gladly accept it."

Bev could hardly pay attention during Mickey's memorial service. Periodically, she looked toward the front of the sanctuary to catch a glimpse of Rita. She looked nothing like the disheveled version of herself that Bev had seen just three days prior in Da-

vid's apartment. Today, to honor her husband's legacy and celebrate his work, Rita was polished and regal. She held her head
high and her attention was focused. She smiled gracefully when-
ever someone at the podium made reference to her or Mickey
and, also unlike the day prior, she shed not one tear.

Bev watched from afar as her friend slipped effortlessly into
her new role as a bereaved widow, but she wondered whether
Rita would be able to handle the constant reminders of Mickey's life—and, consequently, his death—for the remainder of
her years. Mostly, though, she wondered whether Rita was serious about pulling back on her involvement in the movement.
She needed a break, sure, but Bev couldn't imagine that she
could walk away that easily. Then Bev looked up at David, who
was seated next to her, his eyes bloodshot and skin clammy, still
reeling from his friend's death.

She considered these two people in her life, Rita and
David, and how they had both been crushed by Mickey's murder. They were blindsided, and in what seemed like desperate
attempts at self-preservation, Rita wanted nothing to do with
that which took her husband's life, while David seemed to take
some sordid pleasure in knowing that the South was the same
wretched place it had been when he was a child, which only
undergirded his promise to never return. Bev missed Mickey as
well, but learning of his death seemed to have the opposite effect on her—she was more committed than ever to securing

equal rights for every man, woman, and child in America. Shrinking away wasn't an option.

Bev had been thinking about starting a new organization that could raise money and centralize local New York efforts in support of what was happening down south. She would need help, though, so she told David her plans during their shared taxi ride after Mickey's service.

"Social Workers for Civil Rights Action?" David repeated. "That sounds like a good idea. But what would we be doing, exactly? Aren't there already a million small organizations in existence? Are you sure we need to start another one?"

"There are other civil rights organizations, yes," said Bev. "But this would give people who can't directly volunteer in Mississippi or Alabama a way to contribute to the cause."

David waited a while before responding. "Okay, sure. Let's do it," he said. "Can't hurt, I guess."

"So how are you feeling about everything?" Bev asked, switching gears.

"I'm okay. I miss Mickey a lot, but this is my new reality. We all knew how passionate he was about civil rights, so I guess I shouldn't have been that surprised when he decided to leave. I still wish things could have turned out differently."

"I do, too."

"But I really appreciate you being there for me through all of this." David shifted his weight and turned so that he was staring directly into Bev's eyes. When he wrapped his fingers around her right hand, her heart skipped. "I couldn't have made it through this without you, and I apologize if I've been short lately. I just have a lot on my mind."

A lot on his mind? Like what? Bev wondered.

"It's no problem, really," Bev said, her mind still racing. "You're closer to this than probably anyone else we know, being from Mississippi, so I understand how it must affect you deeply. I just don't want you to give up. I really want to make a difference, and I can't do that without you."

David smiled at Bev and released her hand as he gently brushed away a loose tendril of hair that had fallen across her left eye. Bev had made the extra effort to curl her chin-length brown locks before the service, and she was glad she had.

As the taxi driver drove the remaining blocks to Bev's house, she and David sat in silence, his hand once again clasped around hers, and her heart once again doing somersaults in her chest. Maybe Dr. K. had been right all this time. Maybe the man she had been waiting for had been right in front of her all along. Perhaps there was something deeper between her and David than a passion for civil rights work and a fondness for the lemon meringue pie at Shelly's. And maybe, just maybe, David felt it, too.

The cab finally slowed to a stop, and while Bev gathered her purse and the black cardigan that she'd worn over her dress,

David jumped out and walked around to Bev's side to open the door for her.

"You didn't have to do that," she said, trying to mask her nervousness.

"I know, but what's wrong with me showing a friend how much I care?"

"Nothing. Nothing at all." Bev had to will herself to speak. "So . . . ummm . . . about this group, Social Workers for Civil Rights Action . . . Do you think we should have a meeting or something? I was thinking about asking my roommates if they wanted to join, and maybe you could contact some of your old classmates."

"Sure, Bev. But maybe we should get together alone first, to iron out the details." David had taken a step closer to her, and now there were only inches separating them. "How's Monday evening?"

"That sounds good."

"Okay, great. And thanks again, Bev."

Bev was trying to say "You're welcome," but she didn't think David would have heard her. He had wrapped both his arms around her and was holding her close, with her head pressed against his chest. And as they embraced, she could've sworn he held her just a little tighter than normal.

FOUR

Bᴇᴠ ᴀɴᴅ Dᴀᴠɪᴅ watched the Democratic National Convention together on the couch in Bev's living room, a giant bowl filled with buttered popcorn between them. They were watching to catch a glimpse of Rita to see whether, just two weeks after she'd buried her husband, she would stand before the convention and the entire nation watching at home and speak to the gross miscarriages of justice that continued in Mississippi. And they wondered whether she would publicly demand that a suspect in Mickey's murder be apprehended and brought to trial by the people who claimed to represent the interests of the citizens. But Bev and David did not see Rita. They were, instead, captivated by a short, stout sharecropper who grabbed everyone's attention from the moment she opened her mouth.

"Mr. Chairman, and to the Credentials Committee," she

began, "my name is Mrs. Fannie Lou Hamer, and I live at 626 East Lafayette Street, Ruleville, Mississippi, Sunflower County, the home of Senator James O. Eastland and Senator Stennis."

As it turned out, Hamer was born the youngest of twenty children, into a family that moved from Montgomery County, Mississippi, where she was born, to Sunflower County in order to work on the plantation of a Mr. E. W. Brandon. They were sharecroppers—that dubious, post–Civil War distinction given to free Negroes who continued to work on southern plantations, with rights that barely elevated them above slave status. Like most sharecroppers, Hamer lived a hard, backbreaking existence.

On August 23, 1962, Hamer went to see Reverend James Bevel, an organizer for the SNCC and an associate of Dr. Martin Luther King Jr. He was giving a sermon in Ruleville, Mississippi, during which he called all those in attendance to register to vote. And despite the inevitable backlash that faced any Negro who dared to follow his urging, Hamer agreed. "I guess if I'd had any sense, I'd have been a little scared," she said later, "but what was the point of being scared? The only thing they could do was kill me, and it kinda seemed like they'd been trying to do that a little bit at a time since I could remember."

On August 31, Hamer and seventeen other brave souls who had also attended Reverend Bevel's service traveled by bus for twenty-six miles to Indianola, Mississippi, to register. It was a proud moment for the group, as they were taking the step to become "first-class citizens," but not everyone was pleased with their efforts. They were stopped on their way home by city police and state highway patrolmen and forced to return to Indianola, where they were then required to pay a fine before they could set back out for Ruleville. By the time Hamer arrived home, the plantation owner, Mr. Brandon, was well aware of her antics.

"He said, 'If you don't go down and withdraw your registration, you will have to leave,'" Hamer told the Convention. "He said, 'Then, if you go down and withdraw, you still might have to go because we're not ready for that in Mississippi.'" But this strong woman, who was picking between two hundred and three hundred pounds of cotton a day by the time she turned thirteen, was not to be moved. "I addressed him and told him and said, 'I didn't try to register for you. I tried to register for myself.'"

Hamer lost her job and was told to leave the plantation that same night. As a result, several attempts were made on her life in early September, no doubt by angry white mobs who wondered why this uppity Negro woman didn't seem to know her place.

Bev couldn't take her eyes away from the screen as she sat watching this woman who, despite having little to no formal education, had so eloquently put a face to all of the anonymous stories of Negroes living in the terror-filled South. Bev had been smoking continuously while listening, but what Hamer said next, revealing details of the night she was arrested in Montgomery County after attending a voter registration workshop, made Bev drop her cigarette in horror.

"He said, 'We are going to make you wish you were dead,'" Hamer said of the state highway patrolman who came to her cell with two other white men.

"I was carried out of that cell into another cell where they had two Negro prisoners," Hamer continued. "The state highway patrolmen ordered the first Negro to take the blackjack. The first Negro prisoner ordered me, by orders from the state highway patrolman, to lie down on a bunk bed on my face. And I lay on my face while the first Negro began to beat me. And I was beat by the first Negro until he was exhausted. I was holding my hands behind me at that time on my left side because I suffered from polio when I was six years old."

Bev closed her eyes to try to block out the mental picture that was forming, but as Hamer kept talking, the image of her being beaten in the cell grew even more crisp in Bev's mind.

"After the first Negro had beat until he was exhausted, the state highway patrolman ordered the second Negro to take the blackjack," Hamer said. "The second Negro began to beat, and I began to work my feet, and the state highway patrolman ordered the first Negro who had beat me to sit on my feet to keep me from working my feet. I began to scream and one white man got up and began to beat me in my head and tell me to hush. One white man—my dress had worked up high—he walked over and pulled my dress. I pulled my dress down and he pulled my dress back up.

"All of this is on account of we want to register, to become first-class citizens," Hamer said, closing her harrowing speech before the hushed crowd. "And if the Mississippi Freedom Democratic Party is not seated now, I question America. Is this America, the land of the free and the home of the brave, where we have to sleep with our telephones off the hooks because our lives are threatened daily, because we want to live as decent human beings, in America?"

Bev hadn't noticed how tightly David was gripping her hand until Hamer stepped away from the microphone, and Bev finally exhaled. She stole a glimpse of David to her right and was not so surprised to see his eyes filling with water.

"God bless that woman," he whispered.

Despite Hamer's moving speech, the Mississippi Freedom Democratic Party was unsuccessful in seating its delegates during the Convention. In efforts to protect his nomination, President Johnson wanted to avoid upsetting the regular Democrats of Mississippi, so he, along with his eventual vice president, Hubert Humphrey, and the labor union leader Walter Reuther, worked out a compromise with Roy Wilkins and Bayard Rustin of the MFDP. Two of the sixty-eight MFDP delegates chosen by Johnson were named at-large delegates and the rest were considered nonvoting guests of the Convention. In exchange, the regular Mississippi delegation was required to pledge to support the party ticket, and going forward, no future Democratic Convention would accept a delegation elected via segregated vote.

Across the movement, the changes were incremental at times, but they were happening nonetheless. Folks such as Fannie Lou Hamer and others who had been scared silent were stepping up and screaming loud. The threats were still there, as was the fear and uncertainty of what lay ahead, but enough was enough.

Meanwhile, some twelve hundred miles from Mississippi, in New York, Bev and David were working tirelessly to build Social Workers for Civil Rights Action (SWCRA) into a mighty organization that was capable of breaking down any wall before it. Bev had enlisted each of her roommates, and each had obliged. If, in their professional roles, Elaine, Marianne, and Barbara worked to provide access to basic needs—including food, housing, and health care—for the most vulnerable of their patients, it only made sense that they would dedicate their personal lives to the task as well.

David was an eager but amicable leader, who was more

than capable of taking control, but also willing to submit to Bev's direction when necessary. As the summer months faded into fall and things turned icy in winter's grip, Bev grew more and more certain that she could—that she should, even—spend the rest of her life with David. She'd been on a couple of dates here and there (without telling David, of course), but no other man seemed to pique her interest and hold it longer than it took to get through an appetizer during dinner.

She told Dr. K. as much during her session the week before Christmas.

"I bought him monogrammed cuff links," Bev announced happily, as Dr. K. reached over to hand her the ashtray that sat stationed on his desk, though Bev was the only one of his patients who ever used it.

"Oh?" he said, raising his eyebrows above the rims of his glasses. "That seems like a very thoughtful gift."

"That's probably because I spent a lot of time thinking about it. I wanted to make sure I got him something that was unique but still useful, stylish but practical . . ."

Bev could see Dr. K. smiling as her words trailed off. "What? Why are you smiling like that?" she asked.

"It's nothing. You just seem very happy, and that makes me happy."

"I am, Dr. K. I really am." Bev returned his smile. "We haven't talked about it or anything. I mean, we're not officially a couple. But there's an easiness about our relationship that I haven't felt in a long time—or ever, really."

"Really?" Dr. K. said, pausing from shuffling stacks of paper around his desk to look squarely in Bev's eyes. "What about your first marriage?"

"Excuse me?" Bev was shocked by the question. She hadn't ever talked much about her first marriage, other than to say that she had, in fact, been married. She could see that Dr. K. was trying to get her to open up, but there just wasn't a whole lot to say. She got married. She got divorced. Period.

"I've noticed that you always evade the subject when your first marriage comes up. Mark, right? That's your ex-husband's name, isn't it?"

"*Yeeeesss*," Bev answered slowly, trying to determine how this line of questioning was related to her current situation. Mark and David were absolutely nothing alike.

"Well," Dr. K. pressed, "it seems to me that you feel a sense of guilt about the way your first marriage ended. Do you think that's the case?"

"Guilt? What on earth could I possibly feel guilty about?" Bev was irritated. "It didn't work out. I didn't have an affair or do anything other than my expected wifely duties. Why would you ask such a ridiculous question?"

Dr. K. spoke slowly and softly, hoping the timbre in his voice would calm Bev. "I see it a lot with smart, ambitious women like you," he said. "It's not that there's a sense of guilt over the way the marriage ended. But I tend to see suppressed feelings of guilt about the fact that the marriage even existed in the first place. I just don't want you to beat yourself up for choosing the wrong man." Dr. K. peered over his glasses and spoke directly. "Not every man or relationship is what it seems. That doesn't mean it's your fault."

Bev chuckled to herself. Dr. K.'s assessment couldn't have been further from the truth. "I know that," she said defensively. "Mark and I just weren't meant to be."

It was the summer of 1954, the summer after Bev's car accident, when she ran into Mark Martinez, an old beau from high school whom she'd first met at a folk dancing club. They hit it off again and soon picked right up where they'd left off. Elsewhere, however, Bev was still trying to piece her life back together in between brain surgeries, and at the top of her to-do list was to return to the University of Chicago. She was under specific instructions from Dr. Miller to be extra careful until she had the second operation, which would involve the insertion of a titanium plate to protect her brain from injury. "Don't bump your head," he'd told her, "at least until it's protected by the steel plate. And don't blow. That includes musical instruments and balloons."

Bev had also started meeting with Dr. Simon, a psychiatrist

who specialized in head injuries and would monitor her for any signs of brain damage. Bev liked Dr. Simon, and her comfort in seeing him broke the Luther family taboo against psychiatry, as her parents' generation believed that psychotherapy was only for weak people unable to solve their own problems.

As it turned out, Dr. Simon saw no weakness in Bev whatsoever, and he was convinced that she had sustained no brain damage. He wrote a letter to the Admissions Office at the University of Chicago in September 1954 to relay his findings, but school officials disagreed. They believed her injuries were so severe that symptoms would likely surface later.

Bev was incredibly disappointed. In fact, nothing in her life to that point had ever disappointed her as much as the University of Chicago's decision, including the fact that she was still walking around with a small depression in her forehead. She coped with her disfigurement by refusing to look in the mirror, but she knew of no such way to deal with the fact that she wouldn't be allowed to return to school.

Perhaps it was the sting from the University of Chicago's rejection that pushed Bev further into Mark's arms, spurring her to marriage in November 1954, just months after their reunion. Bev was twenty-one years old and certainly old enough to marry, but as far as anyone could tell—including Bev herself—she had little in common with Mark, at least not enough to build a future on. It was less than a month after the wedding, which took place in the backyard of her uncle Harry and aunt Bess's house in Berkeley, California, when Bev admitted that things weren't going well between her and her new husband. A couple of months later, the marriage was over. Mark wasn't even present for Bev's second brain surgery on Christmas Day, the unusual scheduling done because the doctor believed the sooner the surgery, the sooner her forehead could begin to heal.

So, as Bev saw it, there wasn't much to talk with Dr. K. about regarding her ill-fated marriage. She desperately wanted to marry again, but she was also well aware that her first attempt at happily ever after was an utter failure—a failure she didn't care to be reminded of.

"Well, I'm glad you understand that you're not at fault, and I want you to remember that going forward," Dr. K. said, bringing Bev back to the present. "Additionally, I want you to remember that you're also not at fault if you decide not to pursue a relation-ship if you determine early on that things aren't what they seem."

Bev paused a minute, taking in Dr. K.'s words, though she wasn't sure why he felt it necessary to say that. "My mother is coming to town for the holidays, and I'm cooking dinner for her and David on Christmas Day," she said, changing the subject.

Dr. K. took the bait. "That sounds very nice, Beverly. But since you and David have yet to discuss the status of your rela-tionship, do you think he will misconstrue the meeting with your mother?"

Bev hadn't thought about that. She and David had been dancing around their feelings for some time, even as the chemistry between them grew stronger, but she didn't want David to think she was pressuring him by introducing him to her mother. "I don't know," she responded. "That's a good question, actually. Do you think the dinner's a bad idea?"

"Not necessarily," said Dr. K. "If you are at all certain that you and David will transition to a romantic relationship, then Christmas is a good opportunity for him to meet your mother, and I know you would probably prefer to be with both of them during the holidays, right?"

"Right."

"But if you're not certain about the status of your relationship and where it's headed in the near future, you may want to consider putting everything out on the table and simply asking David."

"Asking what?" Again, Bev felt Dr. K. was pushing things just a bit too far. Sure, she was far from a wallflower, but when it came to matters of the opposite sex, Bev had learned to tread lightly.

"I don't know if that's such a good idea," she said. "I'm still not sure how he feels about me, and I don't know if I want to bring it up and risk what we have now . . . Besides, we have so much going on with Social Workers for Civil Rights Action. This country is in the middle of a major shift, and that's what I want to focus on now. Nineteen sixty-five is going to be a great year for the movement . . ."

～～～～

Bev's mother, Lolly, flew into New York on Christmas Eve with plans to stay through New Year's. Her first night in town, Bev took her to Shelly's, where they both had the meatloaf and shared a slice of lemon meringue pie. The conversation was smooth and effortless, and Bev was pleasantly surprised that there hadn't been any arguments or disagreements between them.

David enjoyed having Bev's mom in town, too, and when he came over for dinner on Christmas, he never grew tired of telling Lolly about his work in the movement and with Bev through SWCRA. Bev could sense that her mother had a real affinity for David also, and each time Lolly kicked Bev under the table or winked at her when David's back was turned, she only confirmed Bev's suspicions.

"He sure is a nice guy," Lolly said, as she and Bev were washing the Christmas dishes together once David had left for the evening. "And he's handsome, too."

Bev could feel heat rising to her cheeks. "Yes, Mother, he is. I've known David for a while now, and he is a really great guy. That's why we're such good friends."

Lolly dropped the ceramic gravy tureen she had been wiping into the sink.

"Mother! You're going to break that," Bev yelled. "That was a gift from Elaine's grandmother, and she'd kill me if something happened to it."

"Look, dear. Why don't you put down those plates and come sit down with me for a minute."

Bev hesitated. "I'd really like to get this cleaned up first. It's just such a mess, you'd think that Elaine, Marianne, and Barbara had been here, too, not just the three of us."

"We'll get to it, honey, I promise." Lolly was smiling gently as she sat at the round Formica table and patted the chair next to her.

"Fine." Bev slid open the drawer directly beneath the sink and pulled out her pack of cigarettes and a book of matches before joining her mother at the table. Bev shook two cigarettes out of the pack, lit them both, and handed one to her mother.

"Beverly," Lolly started, as she daintily held the cigarette between the index and middle fingers of her right hand. "I'm starting to worry about you."

Bev sighed heavily before responding. "Please don't start, Mother. We've had such a great time since you flew in yesterday. There's absolutely no reason for you to worry."

"I don't want you to be upset, honey, but I am your mother and you are my child. I am supposed to worry."

"About what?" Bev, growing more frustrated, took a hard pull on her cigarette.

"Well . . . why do you insist on saying that you and David are just friends?" Lolly searched her daughter's face for the truth.

"You're kidding. Is that what this is about? My relationship with David?" Bev got up from the table and stood again at the sink, her back to her mother.

"I can tell there's something more there, dear, that's all. He's a very nice man, and he's so handsome—"

"You already said that," Bev said, interrupting her.

"You're right. I'm sorry. But that doesn't make it less true." Lolly walked over to Bev and put her arm around her. "I'm sorry that things didn't work out better between you and Mark, but you really have to get back out there. You're already thirty-one, dear."

Bev was angry. Was her mother trying to imply that she was turning into a spinster? That she didn't want to get married and have a family? That just showed how much she really knew about her.

It had been almost seven years since Bev had lived at home with her mother, when she and Meredith had worked summer jobs and pooled their earnings so that Lolly could afford a larger apartment after Bev's father, Jack, died from lung cancer in 1950. Like other white, middle-class women of her time, Lolly had been dependent on her husband in an era when many women were not accustomed to providing for themselves financially or practically. And although Lolly had worked briefly when the family had first moved to San Francisco—to supplement Jack's flagging income during the Depression—she saw employment as little more than a brief adventure that would allow the family to rent a house after the war. Once they'd married, Lolly's sisters had never worked outside the home, and she never imagined that she would have to, either.

Jack's death had been a blow to the entire family, and one that took some getting used to. It took time for Bev and Meredith to see Lolly as an authority figure, and Lolly, in response to her new responsibilities, tightened not only her belt but also her rules, holding her daughters as close to her chest as she held her bridge cards.

Naturally, Bev rebelled. She chafed at every restriction, especially curfews on dates and her mother's unspoken demand that Bev and Meredith spend weekends at home with her. The demands never sat well with Lolly's younger daughter, as even in high school, Bev stayed out all night drinking coffee, smoking, and arguing politics. She even started dating college boys and once drove to Stanford University with her date before calling home to say that she was spending the night with his family. Lolly insisted that she come home, and Bev responded in furious haste, accusing her mother of treating her like a child.

Lolly once told her girls that the last question she'd asked Jack before he died was, "What am I going to do without you?"

"Lolly, sweetheart," Jack answered, "you'll do what you have to do."

And when it came to her financial state, she did. Lolly went back to work and planned to sell the family house to get Bev and Meredith through college. She moved to Berkeley, near her brother and sister-in-law, and rented a cheap apartment, as cheap as she could find. And like her mother before her, she took in boarders to make ends meet.

When it came to Bev, however, Lolly could find no obvious solution. They constantly butted heads, and Bev resented her mother for trying to control her life, even after she left home for college and, later, the start of her career in New York. And now, here Lolly stood—on Christmas Day, no less—trying to tell Bev that it was her fault that she was husband-less at the ripe old age of thirty-one.

"Mother," Bev said, loosening herself from Lolly's embrace and turning to look down at her mother, who, at just five feet tall, was a full two inches shorter than herself. "I love you, Mother, and I'm glad you came to visit. But you cannot control me or tell me how to live my life. David and I are friends. If something more is to come, I don't know. But for right now, that is all."

FIVE

AFTER A RELATIVELY quiet end to 1964, racial tensions started heating up once again in the South. But this time, it wasn't Mississippi on center stage.

On the night of February 18, 1965, the scene at Mack's Café in Marion, Alabama, was pure chaos. Following a meeting at Zion Chapel Methodist Church, around five hundred people, organized by C. T. Vivian, an activist for the Southern Christian Leadership Conference (SCLC), decided to protest the arrest of James Orange. At just twenty-three years old, Orange was deeply committed to the civil rights movement, and he had been apprehended on the charge of contributing to the delinquency of minors by recruiting them to work in voter registration drives.

Leaders in Perry County, Alabama, were worried that Orange would be lynched, so they planned a peaceful march that February night. The five-hundred-plus in attendance were to walk from the church to the Perry County jail half a block away, sing hymns, and return to the church. They were intercepted, however, by a line of Marion city police officers, sheriff's deputies, and Alabama state troopers who claimed the crowd was planning a jailbreak.

In the moments that followed, the town went dark as the streetlights were turned off or, reportedly, shot out by police. A melee ensued, and officers began pummeling the protestors with billy clubs, sending them scrambling back to the church.

But twenty-six-year-old Jimmie Lee Jackson, his mother Viola, and his eighty-two-year-old grandfather Cager Lee ran instead into Mack's Café, directly behind Zion Chapel. They were pursued by Alabama state troopers who clubbed Cager Lee to the floor in the restaurant's kitchen. Viola, in attempts to save her elderly father, was then beaten herself. And when Jimmie Lee finally stepped in, the officers' ammunition turned deadly. After attempting to protect his mother, Jimmie Lee was shot twice in the abdomen, at close range.

Jimmie Lee's death eight days later was the final blow for Alabama Negroes who had been fighting for years for their right to vote. As frustrations neared their boiling point, Reverend James Bevel—the same man who had convinced a "sick and tired" Fannie Lou Hamer to risk her job and her life to register to vote—devised a plan to redirect the simmering anger. As the director of Direct Action and Nonviolent Education for the SCLC, Bevel wanted to ensure that the weary citizens of Alabama didn't compromise the efforts of the recently launched Selma Voting Rights Movement by acting in haste. His practical, nonviolent solution was to stage another march—this time leaving Selma, heading east on Highway 80, and ending in Montgomery. Once there, Bevel and other leaders would speak directly to the governor of Alabama, George Wallace, about Jimmie Lee's death and whether he had ordered state troopers to turn off the lights and attack the marchers the night he was shot. Dr. Martin Luther King Jr., who supported the march, also planned to ask the governor for protection for blacks registering to vote, as he hoped the protest would bring attention to the mass violation of constitutional rights in the South.

It was Sunday, March 7, when around 550 marchers started their journey to Montgomery, and all was going well until they crossed over the Alabama River via the Edmund Pettus Bridge. On the other side, they met a band of troopers, as well as a horde of white male civilians who had been deputized just that morning on the order of Sheriff Jim Clark. The marchers were told to turn around and go home, but it wasn't long after the command was given that the angry white men lashed out. There were nightsticks and tear gas, and some troopers even charged the crowd on horseback. On what later became known as Bloody Sunday, seventeen demonstrators were hospitalized after the brutal attack. Amelia Boynton, a leader in the Selma civil rights movement who had helped organize the march, provided global notice that race relations in Alabama were no longer contained, as a photo of her lying unconscious on the bridge appeared on the front page of newspapers and magazines around the world.

Bev was deeply moved by Boynton's image, and she was still clutching Monday's issue of the *New York Times*—with Boynton's bloodied body emblazoned on the front—as she walked into the makeshift headquarters of SWCRA several hours later.

The first few SWCRA meetings were held in Bev's living room. And while she absolutely loved the intimate setting and seeing so many of her friends of all ages and colors gathered there, Bev quickly determined that the group needed somewhere more spacious and professional to convene. The membership roster of the fledgling group grew quickly—from five at the first meeting (David, Bev, and Bev's three roommates) to twelve at the second and twenty-two at the third. David cleverly decided to reach out to Dr. Moses Bierman, the department chair of the School of Social Work at Columbia University. Because Bev and David had both earned master's degrees from the school, David assumed they'd be willing to help. He was right, and soon they had keys to an unused classroom that they were free to use at their will.

The only two windows in the room faced the west side of the building, which meant that during summer months, the afternoon sun quickly heated the small room well past a reasonable level of comfort. The paint on the walls was peeling, and the door had to stay locked in order for it to remain closed. The room was far from perfect, but it was a gift, and it provided space for their organization to meet without distractions. For that, Bev and David were grateful.

When she entered the School of Social Work, Bev walked right past the elevator bank and headed for the stairwell, opting to walk off some of the anger that was welling inside her. As she ascended to the eighth floor, where her office was located, Bev took another look at Boynton's picture and at the arms that were cradling her limp body—arms that likely belonged to some frightened yet courageous man who dared to fight for Boynton's life even as hundreds of troopers had left her for dead. Bev had seen many photos and news reports from the South that upset her. But this one, this image of a *woman* nearly killed because she dared to fight for her constitutional rights? It made Bev question whether there was any human decency at all in Alabama. And it convinced her more than ever that she needed to go and see for herself.

Bev was so engrossed in her thoughts that she ran right into the Western Union messenger approaching the door to her office.

"Oh, I'm so sorry," she said, bending down to pick up the beige envelope that had fallen to the floor.

"It's no problem, ma'am," the sandy-haired boy replied. "I'm looking for a Mrs. Beverly Luther. Perhaps you can help me?"

"It's Miss."

"Excuse me?"

"I'm Beverly Luther," Bev explained, "but I'm not married. So it's 'Miss.'"

"Oh, um . . . I'm sorry . . ." The boy was rattled as he scanned a small slip of paper that he pulled from the front pocket of his pants. "I just have 'Beverly Luther' here," he said. "I guess I shouldn't have assumed . . ."

Bev laughed out loud. "It happens all the time. Really, don't worry about it."

The boy pushed his wire-rimmed glasses up on his nose and offered a slight smile. "Okay. Well. That envelope there in your hand is yours. If I could have you sign this . . ."

Bev reached for the slip of paper the boy had just read, held it up against the wall behind her, and signed her name. "Thank you," she said when she was finished. "You have a great day."

"Same to you, ma'am."

The boy had barely said good-bye before Bev had ripped open the envelope, giving the document inside a quick scan. She stopped cold at the sender's name typed across the top: Dr. Martin Luther King Jr.

Bev leaned her back against the wall and slid down to a seated position to read carefully.

```
In the vicious maltreatment of defenseless
citizens of Selma, where old women and
young children were gassed and clubbed
at random, we have witnessed an eruption
of the disease of racism which seeks
to destroy all America. No American is
without responsibility . . . The people
of Selma will struggle on for the soul
of the nation, but it is fitting that all
Americans help to bear the burden. I call
therefore, on clergy of all faiths . . .
to join me in Selma for a ministers march
to Montgomery on Tuesday morning, March
ninth.
```

She read through the telegram twice more, searching for answers to the questions racing through her mind, but still she was confused. Certainly, she was proud and grateful not only for Dr. King's initiative to take a stand against the atrocities that had occurred the previous day, but also for his foresight to extend the invitation to northerners to join the fight. Alabama may have been a world away from New York, where citizens felt complacent in their more subtle forms of racism, but if acts of blatant hatred such as had been exacted against Amelia Boynton were allowed to continue, to grow and to fester, Bev had no doubt that they would eventually creep their way up the Eastern Seaboard.

But Bev didn't understand why she had received an invitation for a ministers march. She wasn't a member of the clergy. And even if she were, how would she be able to get to Selma by Tuesday morning? That was the following day. And even though she'd given a lot of thought to traveling to the South to get involved at the heart of the movement, she wasn't completely certain that if an opportunity presented itself, she would actually take it.

Bev was still staring at the telegram when she was startled by the phone ringing on the other side of her office door, just a few feet away. She jumped to her feet, grabbed her purse and briefcase that lay askew on the hallway floor, and hurried to unlock the door. Once she opened it she saw David, with his back to her, speaking softly on the telephone.

"Yes, sir. I understand," he said. "I will definitely let her know once she comes in. I was expecting her to be here by now—"

"Who is that?" Bev asked, interrupting David.

David spun around and, upon seeing Bev, told the caller, "Actually, sir, she just walked in." He said nothing to Bev as he held out the phone to her, and as she made her way across the

room to the small desk that held the phone and typewriter—
their only piece of office equipment—Bev had trouble making
out the expression on David's face. Was he angry? Disappointed? Sad?

"Beverly speaking," Bev said, settling into the folding chair
positioned behind the desk.

"Beverly, hello. This is Walter Lear."

"Walter, hi! So good to hear from you! How can I help you
this morning?"

Bev had met Walter in passing at events around the city.
She knew he was heavily involved in the movement; the previous summer he had launched the Medical Committee for
Human Rights (MCHR). The launch of the organization was
necessitated by the fact that in the Jim Crow South, many white
hospitals and doctors wouldn't treat Negroes. Those who would
consider it were often terrorized by the Klan and other racist
groups. This presented an obvious problem when, during protests and demonstrations, black civil rights workers were beaten,
kicked, punched, attacked by dogs, or otherwise injured. They
needed medical care, often as a life-saving effort.

Walter earned his medical degree in 1946 and, in 1948,
graduated with a master's degree in hospital administration for
Columbia's School of Social Work. He had been working as the
associate medical director of the Health Insurance Plan of New
York until recently, when he moved to Philadelphia and was

named deputy commissioner in the city's Department of Public Health.

Through MCHR—which Walter first started in Mississippi to support civil rights work during the summer of '64 before expanding to Alabama and Louisiana—hundreds of doctors, nurses, psychologists, and other northern health professionals descended upon the South. The volunteers may not have been licensed to practice professionally in southern states, but they could still offer emergency first aid to civil rights workers, community activists, and anyone else involved in the movement. According to official MCHR documentation, its workers "cared for wounded protestors and victims of police and Klan violence, assisted the ill, visited jailed demonstrators, and provided a medical presence in black communities, some of which had never seen a doctor." The Committee was also instrumental in establishing and staffing prenatal and other health information programs where they were desperately lacking.

"Beverly, as I'm sure you are aware, a peaceful march in Alabama turned quite violent yesterday afternoon. Armed troopers met hundreds of protestors who were marching simply to bring attention to the fact that they have been denied their right to vote—a right guaranteed to all citizens of these United States."

"Yes," Bev said. "I saw the news last night, and I read the paper this morning. It's so unfortunate what happened. I can't even imagine what those poor people went through."

"That's actually why I'm calling you this morning," said Walter. "We had a team of MCHR volunteers on hand yesterday at the bridge, but we were woefully underprepared for what transpired. There was more resistance, and the attacks against the marchers was much more severe than we expected.

"Tomorrow, Dr. King and other local Alabama leaders are planning to address yesterday's violence," he continued. "There will be another march, along the same route from Selma to Montgomery. And we know that we need to have as many trained professionals as possible on hand to support those efforts."

"So that's why I received the telegram," Bev said, thinking out loud.

"Yes. There was a meeting with Dr. King and the other organizers. They asked if we were aware of any other medical professionals who would be interested in assisting tomorrow. I hope I wasn't too presumptuous, but I have been following yours and David's work in New York, so I passed your names along."

David! Is that why he had looked so upset earlier, because Walter invited him to Alabama? She glanced across the room at him, but he couldn't see her. His head was down, and he was reading the telegram she had dropped on another folding chair positioned near the door.

"But I don't quite understand," Bev said, returning her thoughts to the phone. "I'm not a medical doctor, so I'm not sure how I could help."

"That's a good question, Beverly. I apologize for not making it clear sooner." Walter cleared his throat. "The civil rights movement, as it's currently practiced in states like Alabama and Mississippi, is designed to effect change through peaceful, non-violent action. Unfortunately, however, much of the opposition we face takes the opposite approach. The people who were on that bridge yesterday—many of whom will be expecting to march tomorrow—were badly beaten. That impacts their physical bodies, obviously, but it also impacts their mental state. Above all else, we must be certain that the individuals participating in any upcoming marches or demonstrations are psychologically stable and still committed to the ideals of the movement. We have to know that they haven't been jaded or hardened by recent events."

"And that's where we come in?" Bev asked.

"Yes," said Walter. "We need people on the ground who can screen potential marchers and get an accurate assessment of their ability to participate. The last thing we need is any negative attention brought to our efforts by some angry, bitter Negro who feels as though he must fight back against the police." Walter waited a beat. "Do you think you can handle that, Beverly?"

Bev didn't know how to respond. She was flattered by the invitation, but Walter's comments indicated that she probably didn't understand the movement as well as she thought she did. Her skill and ability to fulfill the task were not a question, but

Bev couldn't fully grasp what it meant to be severely beaten one day, and then sign up potentially to be beaten again on the next. Was she getting in over her head?

"Walter, I really want to thank you for thinking of David and me . . ." Bev said, hesitating.

"Well, it's actually just you now, as far as representation from your organization," Walter said, confirming Bev's suspicions. "David made it very clear that he was not interested in coming to Alabama, but I have reached out to some other individuals, outside of SWCRA."

"I am so sorry about that." Bev looked over at David again, but his eyes were still avoiding her. "I am definitely interested, but I would need to think more about it. Is that okay?"

"Sure, Beverly. But I must let you know that we have already reserved tickets on a flight leaving this evening at six thirty. So there isn't much time."

"Yes. I understand," Bev said. "I will be in touch shortly."

David wasn't listening to a thing Bev said. At least that's how it seemed. No matter how much she described the plight of Negroes in the South, no matter how much she communicated the urgency to do whatever necessary to stem the racist tide, and no matter how much she expressed the need for northerners to get involved, her appeals fell on deaf ears.

"I don't understand why we're having this conversation again," David snapped. He was pacing the floor of the tiny classroom, his long strides taking him end to end in about five steps.

Bev was still seated at the desk, watching David go back and forth. "I don't understand why you're so angry. There's really nothing to be angry about."

"I'm *angry*," David said, mocking Bev, "because you're actually considering this."

"Why wouldn't I?"

"Why *would* you?"

"Look, David, I know how you feel about this." Bev walked over and placed her hand on his arm, trying a softer approach. "But things are different now. The nation is watching. We have the support of people across the country, even in Washington. Now is our time."

"That's great, Bev. But what about what we're doing here, in New York. You convinced me to start SWCRA with you, and now you want to leave?"

"I'm not *leaving*. I'm going where we are needed most right now. It's about priorities, and what's happening in the South can't wait. Why can't you see that?"

"Well, then, think about this woman." David grabbed Bev's newspaper and thrust Boynton's picture in her face. "Think about Mickey. Don't you think they thought it was their time, too?"

"No offense, David, but this woman is still alive," Bev said, grabbing the paper from him. She shuddered again at the sight and pushed down the uncertainty that had been creeping up since she spoke with Walter. How could someone—*anyone*—see Boynton in that condition and not want to retaliate?

"I'm sure she knew there were risks," Bev added, "but that's actually why they need more people tomorrow, to make sure this doesn't happen to anyone else."

"Do you have any idea how ridiculous you sound? You can't prevent this!" David was yelling now, and Bev was taken aback. She had never seen him so visibly upset. "You're dealing with people who have no respect for the law because they *are* the law! Do you think I want to see your picture on the cover of the *Times*?"

Bev paused. "Is that what this is about?" she asked. "You're concerned that something is going to happen to me?"

Bev could feel hundreds of tiny butterflies in her stomach, and she wondered whether, despite the tension in the room, this would be the moment David would finally reveal his feelings for her. She waited in expectation.

"You just said it yourself," David said flatly. "I already lost one friend. I really don't want to lose another one."

Bev was visibly deflated, and she was not at all concerned with hiding it. "Oh, okay," she said angrily. "Well, since you don't want to lose a *friend*, I assure you that I'll do my best to remain safe." She turned from David and started to gather her things.

"Wait, Bev." David, dumbfounded, reached to grab Bev's arm as she walked away. "What just happened here? Are we still talking about Selma?"

"Of course we are. What else would we be talking about? What else is there *to* talk about? Nothing, right?"

David stared at her in silence.

"Exactly," Bev snapped, as she started shoving random papers into her briefcase.

"Okay, something's obviously going on here, only I don't know what it is," David said. "Please tell me what's wrong with you."

"It's nothing." Bev stopped trying to will back the tears that were starting to sting her eyes.

"If it's nothing, then why are you crying?"

Bev looked up at David, at the sexy way his eyebrows knitted together when he was deep in thought, trying to figure something out. "I just thought . . ." Bev started, then stopped. "On second thought, I don't know what I thought, so forget it."

"You're not making any sense." David had positioned his long frame in front of the door, blocking Bev's exit. "I have no idea what you're trying to say, and I know that I can't help you unless you stay and talk to me."

Bev was frustrated and embarrassed. "Talk about what? Talk

about how you just called me your friend, when I foolishly thought that, after all these months, there was something more between us? Is that what you want to talk about?"

David's face relaxed as the lights finally came on in his mind. He stepped away from the door and moved toward Bev. "Look, if I gave you the wrong impression, I'm so sorry," he said softly. "You really are a great friend to me—my best friend, actually. That's why I don't want you to leave. But as far as our relationship, there being something more . . . I . . . I just can't."

"Then I don't understand," Bev said, still crying. "If we get along so well, and we're such good friends, why would it be so difficult to consider being in a relationship with me?"

"I never said it was difficult," David said. "You're smart; you're beautiful . . ."

Bev felt her cheeks warm as she took in the compliment she so rarely received. Intelligent? Yes. Ambitious? Sure. Articulate? Absolutely. Fearless? Without a doubt. But beautiful? She guessed it depended on whom you asked, but Bev knew her upturned nose and freckles didn't fit the standard definition. She was far more often called "cute"—a description she loathed. It meant everything that David saw more.

"Well, what is it, then?" she asked, demanding a more logical explanation for his rejection. "Is it because I'm considering going to Alabama?"

"What?" David was surprised by her accusation. "No, Bev.

I know you well enough to know that when you've made your mind up about something, there's no sense in getting in your way."

David walked over to the windows and stared down to the courtyard below. He watched a young couple lean in for a quick kiss when they thought no one was looking. "Look," he said, turning back around to face Bev. "If we were having this conversation twenty or thirty years from now, things would probably be different. But we're not, and there's nothing I can do about that."

"What would time have to do with it?" As she asked the question, Bev looked down and saw Dr. King's telegram lying on the chair next to her, and she immediately knew the answer. But she still wanted to hear it from David. "Is this because I'm *white*?"

David didn't try to deny it. "Let's not pretend that it wouldn't be an issue, Bev."

"An issue for who? Not for me, and I'd hope not for you." In an instant, Bev's disappointment had turned to anger. "As far as I'm concerned, no one else matters. I, personally, don't give a damn what other people think. You act like this is Birmingham or something."

David narrowed his eyes at Bev. "So you think racism doesn't exist in New York?"

"That's not what I said."

"But that's what you implied. And, no, I may not get beaten and thrown into a river for flirting with a white woman, or even for having one on my arm." David paused to let his reference to Emmett Till settle before he continued. "But I'm not fool enough to think that it doesn't matter. Hell, practically every time we go out, people stare and whisper. I don't want to live my whole life like that. And I certainly wouldn't want to bring any kids into that situation."

That was it. The final dagger. No marriage. No children. No future. It was over before it ever started.

With David no longer blocking the door, Bev decided to make a run for it. Then, with one hand on the doorknob, she turned and said, "You're playing things awfully safe now, aren't you, Mr. Dunning?"

"Excuse me?"

"First Selma; now us. I hope it's comfortable there inside your limited perspective."

"What's that supposed to mean?" David asked.

"It means I'm leaving. I have a six thirty flight."

SIX

INCLUDING BEV, THERE were five volunteers who boarded the plane headed for Birmingham. Their flight was scheduled to land in Alabama at eight o'clock local time, then they had a ninety-mile car ride into Selma. It wasn't the most ideal of travel itineraries, but it was the best they could do at the last minute.

The civil rights community was fairly small in New York, and everyone seemed to know everyone else. So Bev was surprised to see that she hadn't met any of the other workers; surprised, that is, until she learned later that each of the other four volunteers was still in graduate school. One woman, Mary Steinem, was studying social work; everyone else was in the field of general medicine.

Like the Freedom Summer workers whom Mickey and Rita had met in Ohio, these barely legal students were anxious and starry-eyed, ready to go to war against heavy artillery with their bare hands. Conversely, among Bev's peers, age and life experience seemed to bring a heightened sense of reality and awareness that they just weren't willing to ignore. She'd seen that with David, of course, but her roommates had been similarly hesitant. After storming out of the SWCRA offices early that afternoon, Bev headed straight home and called each of her roommates at work, certain that, even while David refused to participate, her closest girlfriends would surely step up and volunteer to use their skills and training for the good of their fellow citizens.

"Alabama? I can't, Bev," Elaine had said. "Work is really crazy right now, and I have a couple of patients that I just can't afford to leave behind. You understand that."

Barbara let romance serve as her excuse. "You know John's parents are driving down from upstate to meet me at dinner tonight," she reasoned. "Maybe next time."

But Marianne was the most candid of them all. "Bev, are you crazy?!" she screamed into the phone. Then, lowering her voice so her coworkers wouldn't hear, "You absolutely cannot go to Selma! You saw the news yesterday. For the life of me, I just don't understand you sometimes!" And then, in more frantic whispers, "Have you talked to your mother about this?"

Perhaps it was the urgency in Marianne's concern, or maybe it was the fact that the two people closest to her questioned her sanity in heading for Alabama, but Bev decided to go ahead and give her mother a call. She lit a cigarette, kicked off her flats, and pulled her legs up underneath her on the couch. Lolly answered on the first ring.

"Hello?"

"Mother, it's Bev. I don't have a lot of time—"

"Bev, sweetheart!" She sounded as if she had just woken up—it was just after nine in the morning on the West Coast—but when she heard Bev, all grogginess disappeared from her voice. Then worry seeped in. "Is everything okay, dear? It's not like you to call during the day like this. Are you at work?"

"No, I'm not at work. I took the day off because I had some things to take care of with Social Workers for Civil Rights Action, you know, the organization I started with David last summer . . ."

"Yes, I remember you telling me about that."

"Okay . . . well . . ." Bev paused and took a deep breath. "I went to the office this morning, but before I could go in a messenger delivered a telegram from Dr. King, and then David and I got into an argument, and then I left, and now I'm going to Selma, and I wanted to know what you thought about it."

Bev stopped rambling long enough to allow her mother to respond.

"Wow, honey. That sure is a lot to deal with." Bev could almost hear the wheels turning in her mother's mind as she searched for the right words to say. No matter the tension or disagreements between them, Lolly always did her best to comfort Bev and put her at ease when she seemed troubled. "What was the argument about?" she said finally.

"What?" Bev was shocked that in light of everything she had just told her mother, the only thing she seemed to focus on was the fact that she'd fought with David. And if Lolly was still attempting to play matchmaker, well . . . Bev was starting to second-guess her decision to call her mother.

"Look, Mother. I didn't call about the argument. I wanted to know how you felt about me leaving for Selma. David doesn't think I should go—that's partly to blame for the argument. But Elaine, Barbara, and Marianne don't want me to go, either."

"Does this have anything to do with that march yesterday?" Lolly asked. "I saw that on the news, how those hateful officers trampled those innocent people on their horses and beat them with their nightsticks. Is that why you're thinking about going?"

"Actually, yes. Dr. King and some of the other organizers decided to plan another march for tomorrow morning along the same route. They think that it's more important than ever to show that the Negroes will not be moved, and they are willing to keep getting back up to fight for their rights."

Lolly was so quiet on the other end that Bev wondered whether they'd been disconnected. "Mother? Are you there?" she asked.

"Yes, Bev. I'm here. I was just thinking. And I think the second march is a brilliant idea. I also admire you for deciding to volunteer. It's very noble of you. I'm not sure, though, why you felt you needed to ask me about it."

"Well, everyone keeps talking about how dangerous it is."

"Yes, Bev. But I'm sure you already knew that." Lolly's voice was calm and even, nothing like how Marianne's had just been. "You're not stupid, and I'm sure you've thought this through."

Bev *had* thought it through. She had been thinking about it ever since Mickey and Rita left for Mississippi, and even more so since Mickey was murdered. The morning's telegram was just confirmation that it was time to act on her thoughts.

"But I just don't get it," Bev said. "The girls, and certainly David, they're supposed to be just as committed to the movement as I am. It really makes me angry that they can just sit back and do nothing at a time like this."

Bev heard Lolly's heavy sigh come through the line. "Beverly," she said, "you mustn't compare someone else's path with your own. You are created to jump right into the fire, and you can fight on the inside without ever getting burned. But there are very few people like you.

"I can remember when you were just thirteen years old," Lolly continued. "Your dad was going on another one of his generalizations about Negroes. You stood your ground—against Daddy, even—and did not give an inch."

Bev remembered the day her mother was speaking of, and so many others like it, when Jack would stereotype people based on their race, ethnicity, or religion. His beliefs were old-fashioned, illogical, and, given his strong faith, decidedly un-Christian. Bev had stood firm as she stared at her father across the kitchen table and appealed to the good she knew existed in him: *You're better than that, Dad; I know you are. Do you even know any Negroes? Do you know any Jews? How do you know those things you say about them are actually true?*

Bev had had a teacher in high school, Miss Frances Parks, who taught American history with attention to and respect for both blacks and whites. It was extremely unusual in the fifties, and it certainly made an impression on Bev. But in the end, it was those frequent arguments with her father that most helped Bev hone her ideas and feelings about inequality. Long before there was a civil rights movement, Bev cared about people disadvantaged by race or class. It bothered her to see talented men and women held down by poverty, poor education, or lack of opportunities.

"Daddy used to call you a holy terror," Lolly said, laughing. "But you must understand that not everyone is as feisty and stubborn and take-charge as you. Even as a girl you had strong opinions and you weren't afraid to express them; you were quick to talk up and talk back."

Bev wasn't sure whether her mother was complimenting or criticizing her.

"Don't you think I disagreed with your father's beliefs, the way he used to make fun of Meredith's Italian friends, calling them dagos? Or the way he talked about the nice Negro family that lived down the block? I am the only Democrat in my family, for goodness' sake. I absolutely hated to hear Jack speak such hateful words, but I never had the gall to stand up to him the way you did, Beverly. And that never made me wrong, just different."

Bev smiled to herself as she tried to imagine her diminutive mother debating with her brothers, Harry and Herman, trying to explain why JFK would make a better president than Nixon. "I never knew that," Bev said. "Why didn't you ever tell me? Why didn't you ever stand with me when I argued with Dad?"

"Because you didn't need me to," said Lolly. "And that is exactly what I'm trying to tell you now. You may be upset that you are traveling on such a momentous journey without the people closest to you, but you don't need them. You've never needed anyone. The road less traveled is often lonely, but that doesn't mean it's not the path that is meant for you. Enjoy your trip, Beverly, and know that I support you unconditionally. You'll be fine, honey; you'll be just fine."

And with that, Lolly hung up the phone.

Hours after the conversation with her mother, Bev had taken her advice and was sitting on a plane headed for the Deep South. Seated next to her was Mary, the twenty-three-year-old social work student from Long Island. Since Bev and Mary would be staying with the same host family once they arrived in Selma, they tried to engage in some general small talk. But, for the most part, Bev stayed lost in her thoughts, contemplating what lay ahead.

Her mind constantly shifted back to the events of that morning, to the conversation with David and the realization that nothing more would ever come of their friendship. Bev wondered, now, whether things could ever be the same—now that she had completely exposed her feelings for him and he, in turn, had effectively dismissed them. And all because she was white.

Bev had spent the entire ride home from the office trying to convince herself that David wasn't some sort of reverse racist, strategically withholding his love from every woman other than those with brown skin. He was right that they went out together quite often, but she had never noticed anyone staring at them or whispering behind their backs. And so what if they did? Isn't that what their work was all about? Weren't they supposed to be fighting *against* the small-minded bigots who tried to deflect their limited views of society onto everyone around them? Isn't that why she, and Dr. King, and hundreds of other protestors would be marching the very next day—to show that they were courageous enough to claim the life they wanted to live, not the pitiful existence that was handed to them?

Just before takeoff, Walter walked back from the front of the plane and handed both Bev and Mary a thick pamphlet. "Reading material," he called it, and he demanded that they have it read, cover to cover, by the time they landed. "Study it carefully," he instructed in his standard no-nonsense style. "Your life could very well depend on it."

Bev looked down at the front cover. *Medical Committee for Human Rights, Manual for Southern Medical Projects.* Bev had planned to nap on the plane—she was exhausted after the long day and figured she needed to be well rested for the march the following day—but she turned to the first page and started reading as she was told to do:

> *In addition to strong personal conviction, dedication, and professional skills, one of the most essential characteristics for Medical Committee Members working in the South is the flexibility and a willingness to listen and accept local leadership. Each person working with the Committee may expect to find himself utilizing his training under unfamiliar legal restrictions and in highly unforeseen situations. Each member should also be prepared to be involved in a wide variety of activities, some of which*

may emerge from his own creative thinking, and many of which will have relatively little to do with his professional training. He may find himself in extended contact with a wide range of people who have strong opinions on subjects about which he may be less knowledgeable, and living in surroundings markedly different from those of his home.

Each Civil Rights project in the South has unique personnel and works with a unique community. Consequently, nothing less than extensive experience in the area to which you are assigned can really be adequate preparation. However, the following pages should provide a useful supplement to your first few days of southern acclimation and continue to be helpful throughout your stay as a guide in what have been found to be the most common eventualities.

Bev had no idea what those "common eventualities" would be or even what her exact assignment would be, but she figured she'd find out soon enough and kept reading.

She had already heard from Rita about the necessity for extreme organization in all civil rights efforts in the South, and the MCHR manual was proof of that. It covered everything from what to pack ("Unusual clothing, or anything else which might prove provocative, should generally be omitted") to what to eat. ("Your hosts will be people who might be taking a risk housing you. They may or may not offer breakfast, and you should use your own discretion before accepting, as the food you eat may cause hardship for the rest of the family.")

And, in addressing the most significant concern for any northerner venturing into the hostile environment of the South for the first time, there was very detailed instruction on how to ensure personal safety, as well as what to do in the event of arrest. Bev read through the list of tips:

1   *Never leave or enter the house in which you are staying when local white people are present to observe you. This will meaningfully reduce the probability of reprisals to your hosts.*

2   *Do not release the names, addresses, and phone numbers of helpful local people indiscriminately, and never release such information to the police. Try to memorize and destroy any copies. Remember also that you are not under any obligation to provide information to FBI agents or other federal officials.*

3   *Never respond in kind to verbal provocation by local police or other citizenry.*

4   *Make no unnecessary trips, especially at night and especially not through or in the white community.*

5   *When you travel by car to unfamiliar places, make sure you have adequate instructions, including a map. If you should become lost, ask directions in a Negro community only.*

6   *For the rare night travel, the bulb in the ceiling light of your car should be removed to prevent illumination of passengers when car doors are opened.*

7   *If you are sitting in a parked car preparing to leave and the police approach, try to wait until they are gone before starting out.*

8   *Fill in several slips of paper with your name and phone numbers of the MCHR and other local civil rights groups. These can be given to local people when your arrest in the near future seems probable (e.g., while visiting an injured local person, you see that two policemen are waiting by your car). In the event you are actually arrested, legal help can then be obtained before you are granted a phone call at the jail.*

Bev closed the pamphlet and let her head fall against the headrest as she studied the plane's ceiling above her. She considered that maybe she should close her eyes and pray, since everything she had just read proved that she would need God now more than at any other time in her life.

She looked to her right, where Mary was sound asleep, leaning awkwardly against the window and snoring quite loudly. She obviously didn't share Bev's worry about what awaited them in Selma. In fact, she hadn't opened the MCHR guidebook at all.

Bev closed her eyes and, like David and Marianne had done previously, questioned whether she was in her right mind when agreeing to go on this trip. She imagined them both, finishing their dinners, perhaps having a nightcap before crawling into the comfort and safety of their beds. Meanwhile, she was some thirty-five thousand feet above Kentucky, en route to what could very well be her death.

She thought back to her last conversation with Rita, when she'd told Bev that she was stepping away, that Mickey's death might have been too much to overcome. Finally, Bev understood. No amount of newspaper articles or television interviews covering the movement can prepare you for the personal experience. Bev hadn't even landed yet, but the certainty of the words written in the guidebook—the underlying notion that yes, she could be arrested or even killed for her efforts—frightened her more than she let on.

The pilot's voice bellowed through the cabin, alerting the passengers that there was only about half an hour remaining before they would begin their descent into Birmingham. Bev closed her eyes again, and she replayed her mother's words in an incessant loop in her mind until she fell asleep: *You'll be fine, honey; you'll be just fine.*

～～～◦～～～

Once they landed, Walter led everyone through the airport and outside, where three cars were waiting. They were driven by other MCHR workers who had been stationed in Alabama for some time and had also participated in Sunday's march. They, too, had traveled from the northeast, but they had driven their own cars to alleviate any transportation issues in Selma, as very few Negroes owned cars.

Bev and Mary climbed into the backseat of the first vehicle, a red 1960 Pontiac Bonneville convertible with a black ragtop and New Jersey plates. Walter sat in front.

"Ladies, this is George Hanson," Walter said as they were pulling out of the parking lot. "He's a social worker from New Jersey, and you'll be working with him during your stay. Your primary responsibility for tomorrow is to screen potential marchers to ensure that everyone allowed to participate is of sound mental capacity."

Bev and Mary nodded their heads in unison.

"Bev and Mary, right?" George asked as he glanced back at them in the rearview mirror.

"Yes," they said together. "It really is a pleasure to meet you, George," Bev added.

"Did you both have a chance to read through the pamphlet on the plane?" Walter turned around in his seat to face both of them. "If you have any questions, now's the time to ask. We normally like to spend more time prepping new volunteers, but we won't have that luxury given the sudden nature of tomorrow's event. There will be a brief training tomorrow morning, before you begin your screenings, but if you have any immediate concerns, I implore you to address them now."

"I'm fine," said Bev. "Everything was pretty self-explanatory." She rattled off a few key points she remembered from the guidebook, just to show her eagerness to work and willingness to follow direction.

"That's great, Beverly. And what about you, Mary?" Walter asked. "Did you have any questions?"

"Um, not right now, sir." Mary was trying to avoid Walter's eyes and instead directed her gaze out the car window, to the wide swaths of empty fields that rolled by them. "I was completely exhausted, so I fell asleep on the plane. I was planning to finish reading once we got to the hotel."

Bev could see the anger rising in Walter's face before he even opened his mouth.

"Miss Steinem, where are you from?"

"Long Island, sir. My family has a home in Glen Cove."

"You live with both your parents?"

"Before I went to college, yes. I lived with my parents and my two younger brothers."

"And do you expect to see your parents and your brothers, or that house in Glen Cove, again?" Walter glared at Mary while he waited for her answer. Bev could tell she was embarrassed.

"Um . . . yes, sir."

"It is imperative, then, that when I give you instructions, you follow them!" Walter yelled, and his heavy voice boomed against the walls of the car.

"This is not a joke or a game," he continued. "You are here on very important business, and that is to ensure and protect the rights of your fellow citizens. You will meet terrifyingly strong opposition, so your task is not to be taken lightly. Do you understand me?"

"Yes, sir," Mary said softly.

"And regarding your obvious ignorance about the lodging accommodations," Walter added, "you and Bev will both be staying with Leroy and Essie Mae Simpson, in the Negro part of town. All volunteers are required to live in the Negro community because we feel that this promotes communication and understanding between the local residents and the outside visitors. We also feel it is insensitive to the generally impoverished Negro community to stay at an expensive motel in the white section of town."

"Oh, I see . . ." Mary sounded suddenly unsure of her commitment.

"Your housing will certainly be less adequate than what you're used to, Miss Steinem, but I assure you that you will adapt rapidly. There will be a toilet and running water, but there may or may not be a shower. Things like washing machines, television sets, and other luxuries may be absent as well. But I know that those things are of little concern to you, right?"

"No, sir . . . I mean, yes, sir. They are of no concern at all." Mary was struggling to hold back her tears, certain they would just give Walter another thing to berate her for.

"Do you have anything to add, George?" Walter turned back around in his seat and directed his attention to the handsome driver, who had said very little since they'd left the airport.

George took another look at Bev and Mary in his rearview before answering. "A little fear and uncertainty is normal, ladies," he said. "In fact, it's a good thing. It means you'll be vigilant about protecting yourselves and everyone around you." Walter nodded his head in agreement.

"As Walter mentioned, you two will be working with me in Selma, so I will be serving as your primary mode of transport around the city," George added. "We will do the majority of our work during the day—it's just not safe to be out after dark—after which I will return you to the home of the Simpsons.

"You will be seeing a lot of me over the next couple of weeks, but in the event that I am not around, you both are responsible for each other. Don't ever forget that."

In the dark, Mary reached across the seat and clutched Bev's hand in hers.

Just then, the car that had been silently following them for the last twenty miles turned on a siren and flashing lights. Bev's stomach dropped through to the smooth leather seat beneath her, and, immediately, the tears that Mary had been working so hard to hold back came flowing freely.

"Are you speeding?" Walter hissed toward George, as he dug into his pockets and emptied the contents onto the floor.

"Of course not!" George was offended. "Don't you think I know better than that? I've been five below the limit the whole time, I've used my blinker every single time I changed lanes, and all the tags and registrations are current."

"I'm sorry," Walter said, more calmly this time. He motioned for George to pull over onto the shoulder of the highway. "I guess we should be expecting this by now."

"Expecting what?" Mary asked. Her voice was frantic, and she held her hands together tightly. Bev wasn't sure if she was praying or just trying to keep her hands from shaking so violently. "What's going to happen to us?" she asked. "My mom and dad said that something like this could happen, but I didn't think it would be so soon. I mean, we *just* landed—"

"Now, listen!" Walter snapped his head around to the back-seat and spoke with so much force Bev was beginning to feel more afraid of him than the two highway patrolmen who were quickly approaching. "You are to remain completely silent un-less you are spoken to directly. And if one of the officers does question you, remember your rights and speak boldly and assur-edly." He looked at Mary directly. "These men can smell fear a mile away, and they will take no greater pleasure than to exploit it at your mercy. You are to be firm and stay strong. Is that un-derstood?"

Bev and Mary nodded silently as the shorter of the two pa-trolmen rapped his nightstick against the driver's side window.

George slowly rolled the window down with his left hand, while raising his right in surrender. "How can I help you, sir?" he asked.

The glow from the moon was just bright enough that Bev could see the patrolman's tight, squinty brown eyes and cheeks that were apple-red from the Alabama sun. He held a dip of to-bacco in his right cheek and paused to spit on the asphalt before answering George.

"First, you can tell me where you're headed to this time a'night, out here in the middle'a nowhere," he drawled. He stuck his bald head in the window and peered at Walter, Mary, and Bev. "On second thought, before you answer, per-haps you oughta hop on outta the car. And that goes for the rest of y'all, too," he said, waving his nightstick inches from George's head.

"Excuse me, sir," George interjected, "but may I ask why we were pulled over? I've been careful to drive the speed limit. I'm well aware of my rights, and I don't see any just cause—"

"Hey, Ed!" the short patrolman called over to his taller, fatter partner who was leaning against the trunk of the car. "This boy over here talkin' 'bout 'just cause'!" He laughed out loud. "This boy must not be from 'round these parts, seein' as how he don't know we can pull over whoever the hell we want to. Ain't that right, Ed?"

"Sure is, Tommy," Ed said. "Why don't you have 'em get out so we can explain how things work around here?"

Tommy stuck his head in the window again. "You heard the man," he hissed. "Everybody out. Now!"

Bev stole a glance at Mary before opening her door and stepping out into the brisk night air. Then, she could hear Mary's soft whimpers as the four of them stood side-by-side behind George's Bonneville.

"What's this about?" Walter asked, speaking up for the first time.

"We got word 'bout some aggravatin' goin' on in Selma," Tommy said. "Heard there might be some folks comin' in from outta town to make a bad situation worse. You know anything 'bout that?"

"No, sir, I don't," Walter said carefully.

"You don't, huh? Well I find that hard to believe. If you ask me, the four of y'all look like a bunch of nigger lovers if I ever seen one." He spat again, and the dark brown liquid landed on the toe of Walter's shoe. "What you think, Ed?"

"Definitely some nigger lovers," Ed answered. "This one here, especially." Ed was standing just inches from Bev's face, and he took a handful of her hair and pressed it against his nose. "She even *smells* like a nigger," Ed joked, his hearty laugh piercing the night.

Bev cringed as Ed's tobacco-stained breath filled her nostrils. She heard Mary's cries growing louder, and she prayed that Tommy and Ed wouldn't direct their vileness toward her. Mary would never be able to handle it.

"Listen." George, who was standing to Bev's left, stepped forward from their impromptu lineup and addressed Ed. "Either you're going to arrest us or you're not. We've committed no crime here, and I don't see any reason for you to speak to a woman like that."

Ed released Bev's hair and stepped away from her, but not before flashing his mouthful of crooked, stained teeth in a sleazy grin. "I'm sure I'll be seeing you around," he whispered in her ear.

Tommy, on the other hand, didn't back down from George so easily. The patrolman stood directly in front of him, calling his bluff while Bev eyed the handcuffs hanging haphazardly from his belt. "So you want me to arrest you; is that right?" he said. "If I was you, I'd be careful what you wish for. Bein' a nigger lover don't get you nothin' but trouble." Tommy turned and, for what seemed like hours, took a hard look at Walter, then Bev and Mary. Finally, he turned back to George. "I'm gonna let y'all go tonight—this *one time*," he said. "But I can guarantee I ain't gonna be so nice next time."

Tommy and Ed marched back to the patrol car, with Ed's laughter still dancing in the wind. Then, as soon as they pulled off, Mary collapsed into Bev's arms in tears.

SEVEN

Traveling from the white section of Selma to the Negro side of town gave "other side of the tracks" new meaning. Even in the dark of night, Bev could see how quickly the homes morphed from symbols of pride and status, with manicured lawns, to rickety shacks that appeared to be ill-equipped to withstand even a small gust of wind.

Relatively speaking, the Simpson home was one of the nicer Negro abodes. It was about half the size of where Bev lived in New York, but it was obvious that it was well taken care of. The white paint on the exterior looked fresh, and a broom propped up in front suggested that the porch remained swept at all times.

Once George put the car in park, Bev and Mary crawled out of the backseat, stiff from their journey and still shaken up from the run-in with Tommy and Ed. They said soft good-byes to George while Walter offered to carry their bags inside. The three of them had barely taken two steps when an array of delicious smells filled their noses.

"Hey, y'all!" A light-skinned black woman with a silk scarf tied over a head full of dark brown curls opened the front door. She was speaking in an urgent tone and waving her arms wildly. "Y'all hurry up and get in here 'fore someone sees!"

Bev and Mary did as they were told, practically jogging the rest of the way to the porch. Walter, however, took his time. "Be there in a minute, Essie Mae," he said. "I'm not getting around like I used to."

Essie Mae ushered the three inside, and Bev could see that the home was as well-maintained on the inside as it was on the outside. They moved through a small sitting area with two plush chairs and a navy couch with small yellow flowers on the fabric. There were no pictures anywhere, Bev noticed, but there was a small bookcase next to the window on the front wall of the house. From where she stood, Bev could make out two tattered copies of the Bible, as well as Richard Wright's *Native Son*, *Invisible Man* by Ralph Ellison, and *Their Eyes Were Watching God* by Zora Neale Hurston.

"Y'all come on in here and have a seat; you must be starvin' after that long trip." That was Essie Mae again, her sexy southern drawl lilting through the small house. And once again, Bev and Mary obeyed her command. "So what took y'all so long? I was starting to get worried."

"We got pulled over by a couple of highway patrolmen about fifteen minutes outside of town," Walter said after walking Bev and Mary's bags to a room in the back of the house.

"Oh no!" Essie Mae threw her hand over her mouth, and her eyes grew as wide as grapefruits. "Is everything okay? What happened? Y'all are here, so I see they didn't arrest you. That's good, at least."

"Yes, it is. They probably just had a record of George's plates, and they probably even knew when we would be flying in. You know, everything that's happening here in Selma is drawing national attention. It's really no surprise that those fools are out behaving that way, just looking for somebody to harass."

"Man, I'm so sorry about that," Essie Mae said, shaking her head. "So how are you ladies feelin' after all that?" She turned to face Bev and Mary. "I know that musta scared you something serious."

"I'm a little shaken up, but I'm okay now, I think," Bev said. "It comes with the territory, right?"

"Unfortunately, yes," Essie Mae said. She looked at Mary, whose eyes had never left the pale blue carpet on the living room floor. "Are you okay, baby?"

Mary was silent for a while, her head still down. Finally she looked up with red-rimmed eyes. "No, I'm not okay. May I be excused? I just think I need to lie down."

Essie Mae, Bev, and Walter watched as Mary headed down the hallway. "That's tough," Essie Mae said.

"It is," Walter said. "But we try to prepare all the volunteers for this sort of thing well in advance. I just don't think she actually expected it to happen to her."

Essie Mae shook her head again. "Well, it ain't nothing I can do about what happened on the highway, but at least I can put some good food in your stomach before you head back out," she said to Walter.

"It sure smells good in here, and I'd love to stay, but George and I have a few things to take care of before the march tomorrow."

"You sure about that?" Essie Mae asked, objecting. "We got your favorite: fried chicken with butter beans and potato salad. And I whipped up a red velvet cake this morning."

Bev just noticed that her stomach was growling uncontrollably. Who cooks like this on a Monday night?

"I'm sorry, Essie Mae. Maybe next time," Walter said. "But thank you for the generous offer."

By the time Walter was out the door, Bev was seated at the small, round table in the kitchen, eagerly awaiting her plate. And as she waited, she was surprised to see that it was Essie Mae's husband who was responsible for the food prep.

Leroy Simpson was on the complete opposite end of the color spectrum from his butterscotch-colored wife, with perfectly smooth skin the color of black coffee. They were a beautiful couple in their early forties, his solid, muscular frame perfectly complementing her ample curves.

"Well, I can't wait to eat," Bev said. "The food looks incredible."

"Just wait till you taste it," Essie Mae said, looking lovingly at her husband. "A man that fine who can cook, too? I'm the luckiest girl on earth."

Bev smiled.

"So you're Beverly," said Leroy, finally addressing his guest as he carried the platter of perfectly fried chicken to the table. "I overheard you talkin' 'bout what happened on the way in. Wish I could tell you them boys were a special welcoming committee just for you, but sadly, that kinda thing happens a lot down here." He offered a sympathetic smile. "But we're honored and blessed to have you here. Can't have enough good folks like you, willing to come all the way down here to help us country folk."

"The pleasure is ours, really," said Bev. "And please call me Bev."

"You got it, Bev," Leroy said, flashing a mouthful of perfectly straight, perfectly white teeth.

"So will the two of you be marching tomorrow?" Bev asked.

"Better believe it." Leroy nodded in Essie Mae's direction. "We already registered to vote. But we know, outside of us, can't be no more than a dozen other Negro families voting in this county. The white folks 'round here just got everybody so scared." Leroy looked at Bev directly. "No offense."

"None taken. But I think it's amazing that you were brave enough to register in such a hostile environment. I'm sure you didn't have much support, even within your own community."

"Here's the thing, Bev. You're from New York, right?"

"Yes, sir."

"Well, up there, white folks may not be invitin' Negroes over for dinner or nothin' like that, but at least they understand we got some sense. We can be educated and have businesses and take care of ourselves. You know what I'm sayin'?"

"I think so," said Bev.

"Like that play, *A Raisin in the Sun*, by Lorraine Hansberry. I remember when it hit Broadway in '59, and it was in all the papers. Even the white critics kept going on and on 'bout how good it was—even though it was written by a young colored girl, not even thirty years old."

Leroy was right. Bev remembered all the acclaim *A Raisin in the Sun* received shortly after she'd moved to New York in 1958. In 1959 the New York Drama Critics' Circle named it the best play of the year, and in 1960 it was nominated for four Tony Awards.

"But down South?" Leroy continued. "White folks down here think Negroes ain't worth the cotton it take to clothe us. Think we all deaf, dumb, and blind and can't see how they been gettin' over on us for generations. Some of us might play along, but not me. I ain't shuckin' and jivin' for no white man who ain't gon' pay my bills and take care of my wife. I know my rights, and I got a right to vote. Simple as that."

Bev wasn't sure what she was expecting when she met Leroy, but she was amazed by this man who, at no less than six-two and two hundred pounds, was a dominating physical presence—and an intellectual one as well.

"So you guys have been to New York?" Bev looked at Essie Mae.

"Just Leroy, when he played Negro baseball for the Birmingham Black Barons. That's where we met, in Birmingham. Then, after the league fell apart and they quit playin' games, we moved here to be close to family."

"That's my point exactly," Leroy added. "When I played for the Barons, the Negro Leagues was the most successful business in the Negro community. White folks say we can't play Major League Baseball? Fine. We'll play by ourselves. Got more talent anyway.

"Then here come Branch Rickey," Leroy continued. "Call himself doing us a favor by *letting* us play baseball with the white boys. But look what happened. Jackie left the Monarchs.

Then Larry Doby was gone, Don Newcombe, Satch . . . Wasn't long 'fore the Negro Leagues was dead and gone, and all the Negro ballplayers was once again dependin' on some white man to give 'em a job and write 'em a check."

Bev nodded. She hadn't ever considered that the integration of Major League Baseball could have produced anything other than positive effects. "When did you stop playing?" she asked.

"In '55. Wasn't much left by then, though. No fans, no real talent. I never was that good myself, but I did play with Willie Mays in '48 and '49. After I quit ball, me and Essie Mae moved back to Selma and opened up a juke joint about five miles from here on a piece of land my daddy owned. It's called the Sweet Spot. Ain't much, but it's ours and it means we ain't got to ask these crazy white folks for nothin'.

"Now, we know all white folks ain't bad," Leroy continued, almost apologizing. "But these ones down here give all y'all a bad name. Like them ones y'all met on the highway? It's a shame, really. They done scared that girl half to death," he said, motioning toward the room where Mary was resting. "She'll probably be on the next thing smoking and headed back to New York tomorrow morning."

Leroy was obviously a man who wasn't afraid of taking a stand and demanding justice for himself and his wife, even without the aid of "good" white people like Bev and Mary. So Bev asked why, as millions of tormented and disenfranchised

Negroes had moved north to places such as New York and Chicago, Leroy and Essie Mae hadn't.

"Well, I got my business here, for starters," Leroy answered. "And I guess it woulda been different if we had kids to think about, but we never could have none—even though we sure had fun trying."

Essie Mae smiled at her husband.

"Point is," Leroy continued, "I just didn't feel like I could leave the rest of the people here. Our friends and neighbors, most of 'em stayed 'cause they didn't have the money to go, or they didn't have family already up north that could take 'em in. And I think the white folks know that, so they're extra hard on everybody that's left. Guess they figured anybody that had a lick a sense got the hell outta here some time ago."

"I guess that does make sense," Bev said.

"So me and Essie Mae, we feel like we got an obligation. The Sweet Spot gives 'em a place to let off some steam after they been workin' all week, cleanin' up after white folks and raisin' up their babies. Me and Essie Mae remind 'em that things can be better. If we stand together, it's power in numbers. We can take back our rights and we ain't gotta be scared to do it."

Bev and Mary were sharing the small guest bedroom, directly across the hall from Leroy and Essie Mae's room. The room itself was pretty bare, except for a small chest of drawers in the northeast corner, a full-length mirror, and a queen-size bed. Aside from her short-term husband, Bev hadn't shared a bed with anyone except her sister, and that had been more than twenty years prior. The bed was covered in pillows and a down blanket, though, so at least it looked comfortable.

Bev had just returned from the bathroom when she saw Mary sitting on the edge of the bed, still dressed, with tears rolling slowly down her cheeks.

"You'll be happy to know there is a shower," Bev said, trying to lighten the mood.

It didn't work; Mary turned and looked at Bev only briefly before returning her gaze to the floor.

"Is everything okay?" Bev asked.

"I'm fine," Mary said, sniffling. "I just think I need to leave."

"Oh, Mary," Bev said, taking a seat next to her. "Is this about what happened earlier? Because, if so, I totally understand how you feel. When that man put his hands on me, I wanted to scream."

"Yeah, I don't know how you didn't," Mary whispered.

"It's because I didn't take it personally. He wasn't trying to attack me; he was trying to attack the whole movement. And in that moment, I was a representative for everyone who marched on Sunday and everyone marching tomorrow, and for everyone who's ever done anything to further civil rights in this country."

"But that's the thing," Mary said, near tears. "I'm not that strong. I'm nothing like you. I could barely hold myself together, and the officer wasn't even talking to me. How am I supposed to survive down here?"

"With my help. And with George and Walter's help, that's how. We're in this together. Just think about the greater purpose. Really, if you think about it, you've already shown incredible strength and bravery just by getting on that plane in New York."

Mary grew quiet again. "That's the other thing, the other reason I think I should leave."

"I don't understand. What do you mean?"

"I feel like a fraud," Mary said, now facing Bev. "My parents are the reason I decided to come. They've always been very racist and distrustful of Negroes. They've also tried to control my entire life, so I thought this would be the perfect way to go against them when I heard Dr. King was recruiting volunteers from New York." She paused before adding, "You're meant to be here; you *chose* to be here. I was just trying to upset my mom and dad."

Bev stared at Mary's face and the makeup smudged around her eyes as she searched her mind for the right words. "Well, all that matters is that you're here now," she said finally, while she purposely blocked out the thought that Mary and her rebellious nature sounded just like a younger version of herself. "The peo-

ple here need you, so I really don't think they'll be that concerned with how you got here, as long as you believe in the
movement and want to make a difference."

"But what if I don't really want to be here?" Mary asked
through her sobs. "What if I don't think it's worth it to put my
life on the line for a bunch of people I've never met? Does that
make me a bad person? Am I no better than my parents?" Mary
pulled a handkerchief from her purse and blew her nose.
"Plus," she added, "I heard your conversation with Leroy. I always thought my parents were the worst people in the world for
calling someone a nigger to their face, or for demanding that we
go to a new church because a Negro family joined. But after listening to Leroy talk, I realized I'm just like them."

"I don't understand," Bev said.

"All those things he said, about what white people really
think . . ." Mary's face was twisted in anguish. "I think I believe
those things, too."

"You're kidding, right?"

"No. I mean, it's not like I've gone out of my way to avoid
Negroes or speak badly about them. But just being completely
honest, I realize I've been harboring some bad feelings for years.
Leroy is so intelligent, and strong, and self-assured. And that surprised me because I don't think I believed that Negroes were capable of that." Mary started sobbing again. "So you see! I *can't*
be here. I'm a fraud!"

"Shhh!" Bev whispered, covering Mary's mouth. "I'm sure you don't want Leroy and Essie Mae to hear what you're saying right now."

Mary looked toward the bedroom door as if she expected someone to walk through it at any moment. "No, I don't," she said. "I'm sorry. I just feel so embarrassed."

"Embarrassed?" Bev said sarcastically. "You feel embarrassed because you thought you were coming here to rescue some poor, helpless Negroes who wouldn't be able to survive without your selfless generosity? You thought you would fly into town for a couple of days and be their savior, and now you realize it's going to be tougher than you thought—that you will have to make real *sacrifices*—and that Negroes are actually good, decent people after all?"

Mary looked up at Bev with red, water-filled eyes, her hair matted to her head on the right side. "I hadn't thought about it that way . . . but I guess so. I guess all those years of listening to my parents spew their hatred rubbed off on me." Mary jumped off the bed suddenly and started putting on her shoes. "I should leave. I shouldn't be here."

"Sit down." Bev's voice was forceful. "What's your plan if you leave? Have you thought that far ahead? Or do you just plan to go home and feel sorry for yourself because you were raised by bigots and you started to believe some of their crap?"

Bev walked around to Mary's side of the bed, picked up her

small suitcase, and began unpacking it, throwing slacks and blouses into the chest of drawers in the corner. "You're not a victim," she said, her voice lower but still strong. "*They* are the victims." Bev waved her hands in reference to no one in particular, or to Negroes in general. "The entire Negro existence is built on backward, unfounded ideals of inferiority and fear that are passed down from generation to generation—much like what your parents have done. Now that you recognize and acknowledge it, you cannot go back to your prior existence and act as though you don't know any better."

Bev turned away from the clothes and pointed her finger toward Mary. "You will stay; you will march; you will work. And little by little you will begin to make amends for the mess your parents made, and for the mess you unknowingly took part in. Your effort alone may not do much, but together, we can erase all those years of hatred so the next generation of Negroes and white children won't even know that American society was once so full of foolish hate.

"Now go to sleep. We have orientation at seven a.m."

The orientation for the new medical personnel and social workers from the north who were to participate in the second Selma to Montgomery march on Tuesday, March 9, was held at Selma's Negro Community Center, with the purpose of acclimating them to the Selma movement and to clearly define the work that lay ahead.

People were streaming in from around the country to participate in the march and show their solidarity for those who had experienced the brutal violence on Sunday. And while organizers welcomed their support, they also understood that some of the incoming volunteers would not be aware of the movement's finer points—the ideals and beliefs on which every demonstration was based, particularly the nonviolent, passive-resistant philosophy.

Father Earl A. Neil, an Episcopalian priest, was the first to speak Tuesday morning, and he directly addressed that point. Neil had attended Seabury-Western Theological Seminary in Evanston, Illinois, and completed his ministerial training in 1960, the same year he was ordained in the Episcopal Church.

Early in his career, however, Father Neil was confronted with often debilitating racism. He had been unable to receive an appointment in his home state of Minnesota, ultimately taking an assignment at St. Augustine's, an all-Negro parish in Wichita, Kansas. After some time, the church lost diocesan sponsorship, which forced it to close. The following inability for the parishioners to integrate into other parishes in Wichita led 98 percent of them to join other denominations. This turn of events caused Father Neil to focus his pastoral mission on resistance to segregation.

Upon joining the civil rights movement, Father Neil whole-heartedly accepted the movement's nonviolent, passive-resistant philosophy. And that morning, just before they would journey some eighty miles to Montgomery, he urged those in attendance to do so as well.

"Maybe you got problems," Father Neil said to the group. "Maybe you got anxieties. But I don't got 'em. I wanna live. And I'm not gonna die because one of you people has a neurotic problem about agitating. We're not here to agitate. If I die I'm going to die at the right time, for the right purpose and the right cause. That's what the movement says. So don't walk into the white community. Don't talk back. Don't give dirty looks. Don't give hatred. Don't provoke. We are not here to provoke."

Bev was in awe of his candor. Here they were, preparing to attempt again the same march that had failed so miserably just two days before, primarily because of the extreme violence that demonstrators had endured. And now, here was this distinguished, well-educated Negro gentleman, urging others to ignore the attacks they were undoubtedly bound to face.

"You will feel disrespected and dehumanized. Expect it because it comes with the territory," Father Neil said, as if he had somehow overheard Bev's thoughts. "You are not to look for validation from white people because you won't get it. You should already be confident in who you are, and in who God created you to be. Then, and only then, can you take the licks without feeling as if you must retaliate or agitate. This is nonnegotiable, so if you're not ready, there's the door."

As he pointed, Bev quickly scanned the room to see whether anyone was headed for the exit. No one budged. But Father Neil wanted to make certain that *everyone* understood his admonition, and that Klan and police resistance would not be saved solely for Negroes.

"My skin is black," Father Neil continued. "Some of your skin is black and some of your skin is white, but in here we're all Negroes, because that's how the white community looks at us." Then he paused, as a wide grin spread across his face. "By the way, we're really all *niggers* to the white community."

Before Father Neil walked away from the makeshift podium at the front of the room, he spoke of Jim Clark, the sheriff of Dallas County, Alabama, of which Selma was the county seat. Clark was vocally opposed to integration, even wearing a button that read "Never" to clearly display his position on the matter. He dressed in military-style clothing and even carried a cattle prod along with his gun and club. He used it, too, once mass-arresting three hundred students who were holding a silent protest outside of the county courthouse. He wielded his prod and forced them to walk to a detention center three miles away.

Clark was also there, supporting Marion city police, on the night of Jimmie Lee's death, despite the fact that Perry County was outside his jurisdiction. And on March 7, as marchers left

Selma and approached the Edmund Pettus Bridge, Clark was waiting. What he had perhaps not counted on, however, was the American Broadcasting Company deciding to interrupt the television premiere of *Judgment at Nuremberg* to show—to almost 50 million Americans—Clark attacking protestors and ordering the horse-mounted officers to charge the crowd.

"Jimmy Clark maybe think he's keeping us from voting," the charismatic priest said, "but he don't realize it's because of him that we will *all* be guaranteed our right to vote." The men and women seated around Bev were nodding their heads in agreement and punctuating his words with choruses of "Mm-hmm" and "That's right."

"If he hadn't been so bigoted and prejudiced and brutal, he would never have made the nation realize what was going on, so God bless him," Neil added.

"Hatred and prejudice are cancerous sores within the body and within the soul, and we have to heal them. But how do we do that?" The preacher paused for effect. "We continue to make it visible because we can treat it when it's visible. We go out there and maintain our dignity and love the people who hate us, and we make these cancers visible for the whole world. Then healing will be the only option left."

The community center erupted in cheers, and Bev looked on in amazement. God bless him? This man who went out of his way to terrorize and torture Negroes? It took a special kind of strength to endure what so many of these people did on a daily basis and still be willing to practice the "love thy neighbor" philosophy that so many others only talked about.

"Let us pray," Neil said, wrapping up the morning's session. "Heavenly Father, we come to You now in unison and complete agreement, that we are willing to stand for the rights that Your Son died for us to have. Your Word says that where two or three are gathered in Your Name, You are in the midst. And we are here, hundreds strong, knowing that You are here right now, ordering our steps and making our way straight.

"We thank You now, Father, for our brothers and sisters, some who have traveled thousands of miles to be with us today. And we thank You that our petitions will not go unheard, that today, the world will take heed to the rights of us, Your faithful children.

"And we pray this now, in the name of Your Son, Jesus Christ. Amen."

"Has anyone ever told you that you look just like Mia Farrow?"

It was shortly after the orientation had ended, and Bev was sitting on a wooden bench outside the community center, eating cold chicken left over from dinner the night before. She turned around and saw George standing there, smiling. And for the first time, she noticed his striking good looks. His skin was tanned—no doubt due to the months he'd spent in the hot Alabama sun—and he wore his thick, brown hair à la John Lennon. It was long and shaggy and perfect.

"She plays Allison MacKenzie on *Peyton Place*," George said, as if Bev hadn't heard him. "You know, the soap opera. You do watch TV, don't you?"

Bev laughed slightly. "Yes, I watch TV," she said. "I just don't particularly care for *Peyton Place*. I'm more of a *General Hospital* girl."

"Oh, I see." George was still grinning, his blue eyes sparkling in the sun. "Well, it's nice to finally meet you in the daylight. Last night was something, huh?"

Suddenly, Bev's mind flashed back to Ed. She touched the lock of hair where his hand had been just hours earlier and shuddered at the memory. "It was definitely something," she said. "Kinda crazy for my first night, for sure." She stood from the bench and grabbed George's right hand with both of hers. "I want to thank you for speaking up for me like that. I know you didn't have to do that, and given the circumstances, I wouldn't have been surprised or upset if you hadn't."

"That's very nice of you, Bev, but you don't have to thank me," George said. "My job is to protect and to fight for the rights of citizens—including white social workers from New York!"

Bev smiled. "I guess we're important, too."

"No, really—you are," George replied. "We're all sacrificing a lot to be here, but we're not just protecting Negroes anymore. Anyone who joins the fight—who dares to ally with the Negro— becomes just as vulnerable. Sometimes even more so."

Bev thought about Mickey and Andrew Goodman. "You're right. I never thought about it like that. But should you really have been that bold? I've heard about things that can happen at the hand of the authorities down here."

George shrugged. "Maybe I have a death wish—who knows. But I do know this: Nothing is accomplished without bold, fear-less action." He paused and motioned to a man standing about ten yards away. Both his eyes were blackened and he wore a bandage around his head. "The Negro in the South lives in con-stant fear and tumult. The people who marched on Sunday faced it head-on. But have they shied away from their greater purpose? Not at all. As long as they are still living and breathing, they're still fighting. That's the position I try to take as well."

"I'm impressed," Bev said.

"Don't be. Besides, the feeling is mutual. And you're no wallflower, either." George winked and playfully touched Bev's arm.

"And just how do you know that?"

"I know you came here—miles and miles from home and everything comfortable. And I know you're *still* here, even after what happened last night. That says a lot. I'm pretty impressed, myself."

Bev and George stood smiling at each other, and she felt her cheeks starting to warm. Then, suddenly, visions of David flashed before Bev's eyes. She had been so sure that she'd found the right person, but he just didn't recognize that she was the right person for him. And while she tried to mask her hurt and embarrassment as apathy, at least internally, it never seemed to work. Each time she thought of David, she was only reminded of how much she cared for him.

But what if this Selma was about more than the civil rights movement? She remembered Dr. K.'s advice and realized that this could be her opportunity to change direction, to make the right decision before things imploded the way they did with Mark. The easy banter with George alerted her to the fact that, perhaps, and if she were open-minded, there were other options besides David.

Still, though, Bev remained focused on the movement.

"Well," George said as he shook his hair out of his eyes and smiled again. "I guess we'd better get to work. Walter wants me to go over a few things with you, so you know what to expect when you're screening marchers."

"Okay, great." Bev put the remnants of her lunch back into the paper sack and placed it next to her. Then Mary emerged from the center's main entrance, and Bev motioned for her to come over. "George is getting ready to prep us on how to screen marchers," she told Mary.

George handed each of them a sheet of paper that he had been holding. The top read "Pre-Demonstration Procedure," and below the heading was a list of dos and don'ts, similar to the one inside the MCHR guidebook.

"Okay, ladies," George started. "Your role is very important within the movement because you are the last line of defense to make sure that anyone who goes out on behalf of the civil rights movement does so with the right mind-set. Our battle is uphill the whole way, so we have to make sure that we aren't giving the white community anything negative to say about us. Do you understand that?"

Bev and Mary nodded.

"Okay. So that means you have to assess whether people are mentally fit to march. And that doesn't just mean determining if they are mentally ill or suffering from some kind of medical disorder that would literally make them incapable of walking long distances. You need to know whether they can march in accordance with the movement's philosophy and whether they can withstand any pressure or violent resistance along the way."

"How will we determine that?" Mary asked.

"That's what those papers are for. There's a list of questions there that should help you gauge a person's psychological state. You need to ask if they've ever been in a violent altercation before and whether they were the aggressor. If they weren't, how did they respond? Did they fight back? Tell authorities? And you need to ask about their reaction to the violence toward the marchers on Sunday and how they would react if the same situation occurred today."

"I got it. So when do we start?" Bev asked, as she looked down at the thin, gold watch that was wrapped around her left wrist. "Are we screening here or at Brown Chapel?"

As she finished her question, out of nowhere Walter appeared and, after saying hello to Bev and Mary, whispered something in George's ear. Bev couldn't make out anything he said, but she was certainly curious.

"What was that about?" she asked as soon as Walter was out of earshot.

"It was nothing," George said, suddenly nervous and fidgety. "We need to wrap this up here and head over to the church. There's been a slight change of plans."

"Change of plans? What do you mean?" Mary's face was wrought with confusion. "I had a couple of questions to ask," she continued. "I want Walter to know that I'm taking my role seriously."

"You'll be fine," George said, helping both of the ladies off the bench. "But hurry, because I think the march will be starting soon."

Now it was Bev's turn to be confused. "So will we be screening today? I don't see how we could possibly have time to talk to so many people if the march is supposed to start so soon. Has the time been changed?"

"At this point, I know as much as the two of you," George said to Bev and Mary as they hurried ahead to the lot where the Bonneville was parked.

Bev picked up the rear and let her mind wander with possibilities. *What did Walter say to George? And why were they hurrying so much now? What caused the change of plans?* She had no idea what was in store once they reached the church, so as she had already learned in her short time in Selma, she could do nothing but expect the unexpected.

EIGHT

By THE TIME George pulled up outside of Brown Chapel A.M.E. Church, there were literally thousands of people milling around outside, clustered on the grass, leaning against the railing on the front steps, and covering every square inch of pavement on the sidewalk and street surrounding the building.

Bev and Mary were working their way through the crowd with George when Bev recognized a group of SNCC leaders near the church's entrance. They were gathered around Dr. King, who was preparing to make an announcement.

"Welcome!" Dr. King said a few moments later, his powerful voice projecting through the megaphone he held and commanding all those gathered into silent attention. "We are honored and grateful that you all saw fit to support this great effort. The people of Selma have been silenced through their vote for far too long, and today we demand that it ends."

The crowd erupted in cheers so loud that Bev half expected police officers to show up and start arresting them for disturbing the peace, well before they could even start the march.

"As we stand here on the grounds of the beautiful Brown Chapel, I must remind you that we are not making this journey alone," King continued. "The Lord has ordered our steps, and He will be with us each step from here to Montgomery."

Again, shouts and cheers rose from the throng.

"Wow!" Mary shouted above the noise. "Can you believe all these people? This is really amazing, isn't it?" she asked, echoing Bev's thoughts.

It was as if the people standing around them had forgotten that on top of the fact that only 1 percent of the eligible Negroes in Dallas County were registered to vote, most of them lived in squalor and were forced into menial jobs where they earned less than a third of what their white counterparts did—if they were able to find work at all. And there was no mention of the racist violence that plagued their communities—violence that constantly threatened to tear husbands from wives and fathers from children, all on the whim of the angry white citizenry. Neither did the people discuss the substandard education system that virtually ensured their families would remain stuck in the same position, from generation to generation.

Instead, there were handshakes and hand claps and an infectious joy that permeated the atmosphere. Bev took it all in and knew, instinctively, that she was standing in the midst of greatness, of history in the making. And even though she could somewhat grasp the monumental significance of what was taking place, she also recognized that she was only a bit player in a massive production.

Local Selma residents understood, too, that this was a real movement from the Negroes themselves. There was plenty of assistance from workers like Bev and marchers from all around the country, but in order for the movement to have the most significant impact on voting rights in Alabama and the protest of Jimmie Lee Jackson's death, it had to come directly from the citizens themselves.

"Now, we know that even while the Lord goes before us, there will be others waiting ahead on us as well," King said once the crowd started to quiet. "Jim Clark and his cronies will probably be looking for us again, just as they were on Sunday. They may be waiting with their tear gas and their nightsticks. They may even be mounted on horses again with pistols drawn."

Bev looked around as King spoke, and while some people, like Mary, were visibly shaken by the harsh reality of his words, most were even more resolved, as if the threat of violence gave them more strength and determination to complete the task ahead.

"But we will not be afraid and we will not be moved!" King shouted. "The Lord has said that all things work together for good to them that love Him and are called according to His purpose. This is our purpose, brothers and sisters, and we accept it willingly and graciously. We step forward with faith, not fear, and we will love those who dare to hate us."

Dr. King handed the megaphone to Father Neil, who then announced that it was time to proceed. Slowly, the crowd of marchers snaked out from the church grounds and onto the street, where Bev and Mary fell in stride.

"So how are you feeling?" Bev asked Mary.

"I'm okay. I'm feeling a lot better since last night." Mary offered Bev a smile of appreciation.

"So you're not still thinking about going home?"

"No, I'm not. I mean, you were right. There are much more pressing concerns here than any issues I may be having with my parents."

Bev noticed that Mary's expression had grown suddenly somber. "What's wrong?"

"Nothing. I just talked to my dad this morning before you woke up. He's convinced that I'm here just to spite him," Mary said. "I'm not, though. Maybe before, but not now." She turned to look at Bev. "This is history. It's the beginning of radical change in our country, and I want to be a part of it."

"I was thinking that earlier," Bev said. "Years from now,

we'll remember this day, marching on this street with these people, and we'll be able to tell our kids that we were a part of
something truly great."

As Bev was speaking, George appeared from behind the two
women and started walking alongside Bev. "I'm glad to hear
that you guys are going to be sticking around," he said. "I want
to introduce you to someone." On his left, he was holding the
hand of a middle-aged Negro woman. Her right cheek was
bruised and swollen and she walked with a slight limp, but none
of that could keep away the warm smile that had spread across
her face. "Bev, Mary," George said, "I would like you to meet
Mrs. Amelia Boynton."

Bev couldn't contain her excitement. "Mrs. Boynton! It is *so*
nice to meet you! I saw your picture on the front page of the
paper in New York, and you are a huge part of the reason I'm
here today." She stepped over and hugged the woman she knew
only from the picture of her battered body.

Mrs. Boynton returned the hug and spoke graciously to the
two young women. "It's nice to meet you," she said softly. "And I
can't thank you enough for taking time out of your busy sched-
ules to come down here and help out."

"It's an honor and an inspiration," Bev said, still gushing. "I
can't believe you're marching today. Are you in pain? Are you
okay to march?"

George interjected. "Mrs. Boynton organized these marches,

and she wouldn't have it any other way. We tried to convince her to rest, but she resisted every time." He looked sympathetically at Mrs. Boynton before continuing. "What the photo in the paper didn't show was the fact that one of the officers actually shot tear gas into her throat. They tried to kill her."

Mary threw her hand over her mouth and Bev stared in silence at the woman in front of them. Bev had never met such an amazing woman in her life.

Mrs. Boynton smiled. "You're so sweet, dear, but I don't want you worrying these ladies," she said to George. Then she turned to Bev. "Yes, I am in pain. But not from these superficial wounds. The pain I live with from day to day comes from seeing my people denied of their basic rights. We deserve the right to vote, and until that right is acknowledged by every person in America, including the folks in Washington, I will continue to be in pain." She laughed softly and lifted a hand to her cheek. "But this here? This ain't nothing. I'll take some more licks if I need to—if that's what it takes to make some change around here."

"That's really incredible," Mary said.

"Really," said Bev. "I'm sure you know how much Sunday's march has already changed the course of things. People all over the world are paying attention now. And so much of that is because of you—a woman. It's incredible."

Spirits among the marchers were high as they approached the Edmund Pettus Bridge, just six blocks from where they started at Brown Chapel. There was a soft chorus of "We Shall Overcome" working its way from the back of the crowd to the front, emboldening the marchers even as they approached the place where hundreds of them had been battered and beaten two days before.

Bev, Mary, and George were just a few rows from the front of the pack, which meant they could see everything well before the marchers toward the back. It wasn't surprising, then, that they were the earliest to feel the lumps rise in their throats as they walked across the bridge and looked down to where Highway 80 stretched on for miles. All they could see were police cars with their lights flashing and troopers standing guard, shotguns at the ready.

You'll be fine, honey. You'll be just fine. Bev silently recited her mother's words, once again searching for peace in what seemed like imminent danger.

"Y'all best head on back where you came from!" Jim Clark stepped away from the rest of his trigger-happy posse, hand on his holstered gun, and shouted to the protestors once they were close enough to hear.

Still, slowly but ever so surely, they marched forward. *You'll be fine, honey. You'll be just fine.*

"Listen here, all you niggers and nigger lovers!" Clark shouted again. "Y'all don't have no business here! I've done my warnin', and if y'all don't turn back we will be forced to take action!"

Then, as if on cue, Dr. King turned his back to Clark, faced the crowd, and raised his right hand, commanding everyone to stop walking. Bev could hear grumbles in the crowd as people asked what was going on.

"Brothers and sisters," Dr. King said through his megaphone, "it is time for us to pray." Dr. King motioned for Reverend James Bevel and Hosea Williams, two SCLC leaders, to stand next to him on each side. Together, the three kneeled on the ground, and in silent obedience, all 2,500 of the marchers did as well. Bev wasn't sure why they were stopping to pray as opposed to pushing forward—she had never heard or read anything about this reaction before—but she, too, bent in prayer position.

"Lord, we thank you for this beautiful day," Dr. King started, "and we thank you that your angels are watching over us and protecting us right now. We thank you that no weapon formed against us in the hands of our enemies shall prosper. And, Lord, we pray for Jim Clark and the rest of the men on the other side of the bridge who want only to harm us as we seek to do your will. Forgive them, Lord, for they know not what they do."

Bev squeezed her eyes shut and offered her own silent prayer that, while they were pausing to pray, their enemies would keep their distance on the far side of the bridge.

"Lastly," Dr. King added, "as we return to Selma, I ask that you touch each and every one of the men and women here. Give them Your peace, Lord, Your peace that surpasses all understanding and help them to be comforted by the fact the battle is already won. Amen."

Return to Selma? Bev was dumbfounded. And she wasn't the only one.

"I drove all the way from Cleveland to be here," Bev heard a woman walking in front of her say. "Dr. King is gonna have to explain this. I came to march, and I expect to march."

The woman next to her nodded in agreement. "He asking for people from up north to come support his work in the South, but he don't need no support for praying. I'm sure he do just fine with that on Sunday mornings."

The women both laughed and shook their heads.

Bev looked over at George, who appeared to be in deep thought. She thought surely he would know what was going on, since he had been working in Selma for months before Bev and Mary arrived.

"What's going on, George?" Bev asked him, clearly agitated. "Why are we turning around?"

"I'm not really sure, Bev." He rubbed his forehead and let out a deep sigh. "I don't think anyone knows except those men up there." He pointed in the direction of Dr. King.

"Well . . . why don't you go and *ask* them?"

It seemed like perfect sense to Bev. How else would anyone find out what was going on if they didn't ask. George, on the other hand, didn't see it that way. "I'm sure they'll tell us when we need to know," he replied.

That was unacceptable to Bev. "These people are here for a reason!" she hissed, careful not to let anyone overhear. "They need to know why they're not allowed to follow through on their goal. And if you don't want to find out, I'll go ask myself."

Bev started to make her way through the crowd when George grabbed her by her elbow and gently pulled her back. "Fine," he said forcefully, looking directly into her eyes. "In case you haven't noticed, there are certain protocols around here. You can't just go waltzing up there asking questions. Wait here, and I'll see what I can find out. Maybe Walter knows something."

Bev hadn't meant to upset George. She just believed that she, along with all of the other marchers, had a right to know why plans had changed without notice. Dr. King and the other organizers couldn't have been afraid of confronting Jim Clark again. They planned the second march with the sole intent of bringing further attention to what had happened on Sunday. There had to have been something deeper going on, and as she watched George and Walter whispering back and forth, reminiscent of the scene back at the community center, she realized that there was.

After the violence during the first Selma-to-Montgomery march, Dr. King and the SCLC attempted to obtain a court order from Federal District Court Judge Frank Johnson that would prohibit Clark and other troopers from bothering the marchers on Tuesday. But instead, on the urging of George Wallace, the governor of Alabama, Johnson issued a federal injunction against marching until a hearing could be held on the matter at a later time.

As a result, Dr. King felt it best to avoid breaking any laws or upsetting local politicians he'd reached an agreement with, so Tuesday's march became a symbolic gesture, as he stopped the demonstrators before they reached the wall of troopers beyond the bridge.

Apparently, he made the right decision. President Johnson, who had previously refused to introduce a voting rights bill in Congress, was in complete support of Dr. King's restraint and was finally spurred to take action. Following the march, Johnson issued a statement imploring all Americans to "join in deploring the brutality with which a number of Negro citizens of Alabama were treated when they sought to dramatize their deep and sincere interest in attaining the precious right to vote.

"The best legal talent in the Federal Government is engaged in preparing legislation which will secure that right for every American," the statement continued. "I expect to complete work on my recommendations by this weekend and shall dispatch a special message to Congress as soon as the drafting of the legislation is finished.

"The Federal District Court in Alabama has before it a request to enjoin State officials from interfering with the right of Alabama citizens to walk from Selma to Montgomery in order to focus attention on their efforts to secure the right to register and vote. I have directed the Justice Department to enter the case as a 'friend of the court' so that it can present its recommendations and otherwise assist the court in every manner in resolving the legal issues involved in the case."

Back on the grounds of Brown Chapel, Dr. King addressed the crowd, explaining the turn of events. He apologized to the marchers and asked everyone to stay in Selma and join him one last time, for a final march that would be conducted with full local and federal backing.

Bev was standing near the front of the church, right at the base of the brick steps that led to the entrance, and before she could walk away to find Mary and George, Dr. King had bounded down the steps and was standing in front of her.

"Dr. King," she said, not wanting to be rude, "I'm Beverly Luther from New York, and I must tell you that it is an honor to be here working with you toward equal rights for the Negro citizens of Selma."

Dr. King grabbed Bev's hand and pulled her into an embrace. "Thank you so much for coming," he said as he stepped back to take another look at her. "Beverly Luther . . . Beverly Luther . . . Ah, yes, the social worker. Walter has told me a lot about you, and it is a pleasure to meet you in person."

Bev was shocked that he actually knew who she was. "No, sir, the pleasure is mine. I was just happy to be invited."

"Of course," Dr. King said. "Most people don't realize how important your role is in the movement, but everything we do is based on the premise that everyone follows the same principles. Without that truth, no progress could ever be made." By this time, there were at least a dozen other people standing around Dr. King, waiting for their chance to introduce themselves or otherwise get close to the great leader. He smiled and thanked everyone for their patience before turning back to Bev. "I apologize that things didn't turn out the way you might have hoped today—the way I had hoped," he said. "But I do hope you'll stay with us a little longer."

Bev, still in shock, spun around and ran right into George. "Looking for me?" he asked.

"I was, actually," Bev said. "I need to apologize for my behavior on the bridge. I just got so caught up in all the emotion, and, well . . . I may need to bridle my tongue a bit."

"No need to apologize, Bev. There's a lot of excitement and uncertainty. You're passionate. There's nothing wrong with that. I actually think it's a very attractive quality."

George was smiling and Bev was blushing again. "Okay,

good. I just don't want you to think that I have a problem with authority. I really understand that everything within the movement operates under strict structure and order, and I am not trying to go against that in any way."

"It's fine," George said, laughing. "Relax." He stepped behind Bev and put both of his hands on her shoulders, giving them a gentle rub. "So . . ." George continued. "I saw you talking to Dr. King. Any chance you're gonna stay in Selma a little longer?"

Bev barely heard the question, as she was still processing the shock of George's massage. She wasn't sure if George was being friendly or if there was something more behind his gesture. It was both surprising and confusing, but she still couldn't deny the pleasure of his touch. "Yes, I'm staying," she said finally. "There's nowhere else I'd rather be."

After leaving the Brown Chapel, Bev, Mary, and a large group of other marchers decided to go to the Sweet Spot for dinner.

Located on the edge of town, just before paved streets gave way to miles and miles of open land, the Sweet Spot was little more than a renovated barn with a gravel parking lot. But you couldn't tell that from the line of people snaked outside the front door, waiting for a table. In fact, when Bev and Mary arrived, Leroy was setting up folding tables in the back to make room for the rush of people.

"Hey, y'all!" Essie Mae squealed when she saw Bev and Mary. "I'm glad y'all could make it! Come with me."

Essie Mae led them to a table in the back near the jukebox, which was playing a continuous stream of Motown. "Y'all sit right here," she said, "and I'll be right back."

Bev and Mary settled into their seats, and when Essie Mae returned, she placed two prefilled glasses on the table. Mary didn't hesitate before taking a long drink. "Yum!" she said. "This is delicious! What is this?"

Essie Mae laughed. "It's just tea, girl. House specialty."

"I've had tea in New York, and it never tastes like this."

"That's 'cause we make it nice and sweet," Essie Mae said.

"Oh, I get it!" Mary exclaimed, like a kid who'd just learned to read. "Like the Sweet Spot!"

Essie Mae laughed again. "Exactly. Now I got something else special for y'all. If y'all thought the chicken was good last night, just wait." She winked and disappeared into the kitchen.

Bev smiled and pulled a cigarette from her purse. "I love her," she said to Mary.

"I know. I wish I could stay for the next march, but . . . I just don't know. I told my professors I was only going to be gone a few days, so I really need to get back. And I have this internship . . ."

"If you think it would help, I'd be happy to write a letter or call your professors and let them know you're working with me,"

Bev offered. "I would think that this experience would be more valuable than some standard hospital internship."

"Thanks," Mary said, "I'll have to think about it." She looked around the busy dining room. "There are a ton of people still here. Do you think they're all going to stay?"

"I'm not sure," Bev said, following Mary's gaze around the room. There was standing room only, and there were just as many whites as Negroes in the building. Bev saw several white ministers who had traveled to Selma from the Northeast, including James Reeb, a Unitarian minister from Boston.

"Well, if I stay, what will we do every day until the next march?"

Bev turned her focus back to Mary. "I heard some of the SNCC leaders talking about making house visits to register voters. I think they're going to organize car groups to go into the nearby counties."

"Sounds like it may be a good opportunity for you to spend more time with George, huh?"

"What?" Bev almost choked on her cigarette.

"Come on, Bev," Mary said, smiling. "I know you've noticed how he looks at you. We all have."

Bev didn't let on about her own thoughts, thoughts that maybe there was some chemistry between her and George. "I haven't noticed a thing," Bev said. "I'm here for the movement. And it's clear that there's still a lot of work to be done. Can you

believe Dr. King?" she asked, taking another draw on her cigarette. "He's just so smart. Staging a symbolic march that toes the
line of legality without stepping over it? Brilliant."

At that moment, Bev and Mary looked up at the same time
to see George standing at their table, holding three plates of
smothered pork chops. "Is it okay if I join you?" he asked.

"Sure!" Mary exclaimed. She grinned at the two of them
while Bev slid over to make room for George. "Bev's just talking
about the march today, how she thought it was a really good idea."

"Yeah, I agree." George nodded. "A lot of people outside the
movement forget that we can't operate outside the laws that gov-
ern us. We're trying to *change* the laws—not go against them."
He paused. "I truly believe the reason Dr. King and Mrs. Boynton, and so many other figures within the movement, have become such sympathetic figures is because people around the
country—around the world, even—know that they are being
treated unjustly. When they are beaten or jailed or killed, people can see that there is no just cause or reason for it to happen.
But if ever we were to commit any illegal action, small as it may
be, that would be the end of our work."

"Because you can't effect real change without the sympa-
thies of others," said Bev.

"Right," George answered.

"Especially those in Washington."

"Exactly."

"Speaking of Washington," Bev said as she took a bite of the corn bread on her plate, "how do the leaders feel about President Johnson's involvement? Do they think he's doing enough for Negro rights?"

"Of course not," George answered. "He's been evasive about a lot of the issues—talking a lot but doing little. But we're confident that's going to change soon. The whole world is paying attention to Selma right now. There's no way he can sit back and do nothing."

"Yeah. It's just unfortunate that we need another bill that solely covers voters' rights. You would think the Civil Rights Act last year would have covered everything."

George laughed out loud. "White southerners will take any opportunity they can to continue to oppress Negroes in hopes of keeping their lifestyles the same. If there isn't a written law that explicitly forbids unfair treatment, we are well aware that it will continue to happen."

The three of them sat quietly, eating their pork chops and greens, when Mary broke the silence. "There's a dance floor over there," she said as she motioned toward the front of the restaurant with her fork. "Why don't you guys go dance?"

"Absolutely not," Bev said, without taking her eyes off her plate.

George smiled. "It doesn't sound like a bad idea to me, but I can't go alone," he said, nudging Bev's arm.

As Bev finished her food, she could feel Mary's stare from across the table. She hesitated for another moment before deciding she didn't have any real reason not to go. "Fine," she said finally.

Immediately after she stood up, though, she regretted her decision. "There's no one else dancing," Bev whispered, as George led her toward the front.

"That's funny," George said, "but I never pegged you as the type to follow the crowd."

"You really think you know a lot about me, don't you?" Bev asked jokingly.

"Not really," said George. "Not yet, anyway."

For the third time, Bev felt flattered by George's words, and this time she was sure about the romantic insinuation.

"Not yet? You're pretty presumptuous."

"I am. But considering how well we've gotten along so far, I didn't think it would be too far-fetched to assume you'd go out on a date with me once we got back to New York."

"A date?" Bev pretended that she was thinking long and hard about his request. "I think I may be able to make that happen."

Bev smiled and allowed George to wrap his arms around her as they swayed back and forth to "My Guy" by Mary Wells. She closed her eyes and let herself drift away from the moment, from the romantic tension with David in New York and the racial tension simmering in Selma. She imagined that life could be as comfortable and as easy as she felt in George's arms. He had a disarming way about him that made Bev feel it was okay to let her tough veneer just melt away. Then, as she was imagining where he would take her when they met again in New York, she opened her eyes and saw something frightening.

James Reeb and two other ministers were standing outside talking when a dusty pickup swung into the parking lot. Three white men jumped from the bed of the truck and started shouting at the ministers. Bev could tell from the way Minister Reeb held up his hands that he was trying to calm the strangers down, but within seconds, the three men were beating Reeb and the other two ministers with clubs.

The scene played out so quickly, Bev hardly had time to react. Finally, she pulled herself away from George and pointed frantically out the front window of the Sweet Spot. "Look!" she exclaimed. "Those men! *Do* something!"

George and several other men who were seated near the front and had witnessed the attack ran out the door simultaneously, but the damage had already been done. As the pickup peeled out of the parking lot, kicking up bits of gravel in its wake, the three ministers were sprawled out on the ground in pools of their own blood. The other two men who ran out of the Sweet Spot with George happened to be workers with MCHR, so they started inspecting wounds and performing CPR. But

Minister Reeb, with multiple serious head wounds, was in the worst shape by far.

"He needs an ambulance!" one man shouted. "Someone call for an ambulance!"

"None of the hospitals will send anyone out here to pick him up," George said. "They wouldn't dare come to the Negro side of town to help a white man who marched for Negro voting rights."

And as Bev watched in horror, George declared, "I'll just take him to the hospital myself."

NINE

"You haven't packed your bags yet, so I guess you've decided to stay." Bev was seated at the Simpsons' kitchen table early Wednesday afternoon, having a cup of coffee and a cigarette, when Mary walked in, looking more pleasant than usual.

She sat down at the table across from Bev. "I talked to my parents last night," she said. "They were upset that I came in the first place, but now that I've decided to stay even longer, they've threatened to cut me off financially. They said I should be in school and that I was throwing my life away to help a bunch of stupid niggers."

Bev was waiting for the good news, the news that would explain why Mary still looked so happy. "Wow, I can't believe that," she said. "That must be really hard."

"Not really. My parents have always been clear about their beliefs regarding Negroes, no matter how ugly. Their reaction to my decision was just confirmation that I'm doing the right thing. It feels good to finally have some real direction."

"So you're sure you're okay with this?"

"Positive."

"That's great, Mary," Bev said. "I admire your courage." She paused, then added, "But what are you going to do about money?"

Mary looked down at her fingernails, "I don't know, honestly. That's my one concern. I'll just take it one day at a time, I guess. I'm sure I can find a waitressing job or something once we get back home to help me pay my last semester's tuition."

"Well," Bev said, "don't worry about anything while we're here; I've got you covered. And when we get back to New York, I'll make some calls and see if I can get you a paid internship or something better than waiting tables."

"Oh my gosh, Bev! Thanks so much!" Mary jumped up and raced around the table to give Bev a huge hug. "I'm so glad we were able to meet and spend so much time together on this trip. You have no idea how much your support means to me."

Bev laughed. "It's fine, really. I'm glad I could help."

While the two were still embracing, the door that led from the kitchen to the backyard opened, and Leroy stepped through, his hands caked with dirt. "How y'all doing today?" he asked with a grin. "Had I known y'all was up and movin' around, I'da had y'all come help me plant my vegetables."

"You have a garden back there?" Mary asked, standing to peer out the window.

"Yes, ma'am. By the end of the growing season I'll have cucumbers, squash, potatoes, cabbage, a few turnip greens, and some tomatoes." He made his way over to the sink and started scrubbing the soil off his hands. "Y'all ever had tomatoes fresh from the garden?" he called over his shoulder.

"No, sir," Bev said, smiling. "I may have to come back down when they're ready so I can try some."

"You really ought to," Leroy replied. "I'm tellin' you, ain't nothin' like it. So sweet, you can pick 'em up and bite 'em like an apple."

He dried his hands and leaned back against the sink, facing Bev and Mary. "By the way, anybody heard anything 'bout that fella that got jumped outside the Sweet Spot yesterday evening? I was in the kitchen but I heard he got whupped so good he had to go to the hospital."

"Yeah," Bev said, suddenly somber as she thought of Minister Reeb. "They think it was the Klan, but nobody's really sure yet. George drove him to the hospital, though, so we can ask when he comes to pick us up later."

"That's a shame," Leroy said, shaking his head. "And that's why I make sure to keep my insurance around."

"Insurance?" Bev asked.

"Yep," Leroy said, motioning to a hunting rifle propped up behind the refrigerator. "Some crazy white boys might think about comin' by here looking for trouble, but I got me some insurance that says they ain't gon' stay too long if they do."

Mary was visibly confused. "But what about the nonviolent philosophy? Why do you need a gun?"

"Why?" Leroy laughed so loud that Bev and Mary jumped in their seats. "It's simple, really," he said. "I ain't trying to be no sittin' duck."

Leroy walked over to the table and sat down with Bev and Mary. "Listen, Dr. King is a real smart man," he said. "He knows that in order for the Negro to make any progress with the white man, we got to be on our best behavior. We can't give 'em no more ammunition than they think they got us on already."

Bev nodded in agreement with his simple logic. It made sense.

"When folks around the country see innocent Negroes gettin' beat up for no good reason *and* they ain't fightin' back, that gets their attention. Makes 'em question everything goin' on down here. But soon as somebody was to get up and raise so much as a finger against them troopers or police, we'd just be the same animals that need tamin' like the white folks say. Dr. King knows that."

Leroy paused and his face grew stern. "But at my house, ain't no cameras or reporters. Somebody come 'round here, I got to be able to protect me and my wife, period. This ain't no march or no protest. This is my life. My home. Medgar Evers got shot and killed in his own driveway. That ain't gon' happen around here."

"Do most of the Negroes around here have guns?" Bev asked.

"I can't say for sure, but it's probably more than you think."

"I had no idea," Bev said.

"Most people don't. So tell me, where y'all headed to today?" Leroy asked, switching gears. "I see y'all plannin' to stick around till the next march."

"We're not sure when the next march will be held," Bev said, "but in the meantime, we're going out into the communities to try to convince people to register to vote."

"Ooh-wee!" Leroy let out a low whistle. "Best of luck, but I can tell you now that ain't gon' be no easy task. Most of these folks you gon' come across ain't too keen on white folks no way. Then you gon' try to tell 'em to put their life on the line for the chance to vote?"

"Is it that bad?" Bev asked.

"You better believe it—"

A knock at the door interrupted Leroy. "One second, ladies," he said to Bev and Mary.

Leroy opened the door, and Walter walked in, rubbing his forehead, a look of exhaustion and worry clouding his face.

"Good to see you, man," Leroy said. "Everything okay?"

"Not exactly. Do you mind if I have a seat?"

"Of course." Leroy waved toward the kitchen. "I was just fixin' to make some turkey sandwiches. You look like you could use one yourself."

Walter ambled toward the kitchen table. "No thanks, Leroy. I don't have much of an appetite."

"What's going on, Walter?" Bev asked. "We weren't expecting to see you today."

"I wasn't expecting to be here." Walter sighed and took a long look at both Bev and Mary before continuing. "Yesterday, when George offered to take James Reeb to the hospital after he was beaten, they were turned away here in Selma."

"Why?" Bev asked. "He's white. And so is George."

"Yes. But it was evident he had participated in the march, so they refused to treat him. After they left, George had to take him to Burwell Infirmary, the Negro hospital, but based on Minister Reeb's wounds, the head of the facility said he would need to see a neurologist."

Bev remembered how lucky she had been that a neurologist just happened to be at the hospital when she was taken in after her accident. "So what does that mean?" she asked. "Was someone else in Selma willing to treat him?"

"No," Walter said flatly. "He had to be transported to Birmingham. An ambulance from a local Negro funeral home offered to take him, and George followed behind in his car. On the way, the ambulance had a flat tire and there was a delay from some local officials who had promised to help Minister Reeb get to Birmingham as quickly as possible. By the time he was admitted, it had already been hours since the attack."

Bev's head was spinning as Minister Reeb being beaten replayed in her mind. "So how is he doing now?" she asked.

"I talked to George after he was admitted. He said the doctors weren't making any promises, but they planned to do emergency brain surgery. He made it through the night, but he's on life support."

"I guess all we can do is trust the doctors, but if he made it through the night, maybe that's a good sign," Bev said. Then she looked over at Walter and saw that his facial expression still hadn't changed. Something else had to be wrong. "What is it, Walter?" she asked.

Walter hesitated. His eyes were shifting from the table to the floor, as if he didn't want to look directly at Bev. "It's George," he said finally.

"What about him?" Bev sunk back into her chair, fearing the worst.

"After Minister Reeb was taken into surgery, George called

to tell me that he was about to drive back to Selma," Walter said slowly.

"Okaaay . . ." Bev said impatiently.

"And I haven't heard from him since," Walter snapped. "I have no idea where he is."

A silence fell over the kitchen.

"But it hasn't even been twenty-four hours yet," Mary said, after a few uncomfortable moments. "Should we really be that worried this soon?"

Walter laughed sarcastically at her naïveté. "Dear, we're talking about a civil rights volunteer in Alabama in 1965."

Bev's mind immediately flashed to the conversation she'd had with Rita Schwerner almost a year before, how she'd said that no one—not even the police—knew where Mickey was. And how, despite their wishes and prayers for his safe return, he had been dead all along.

Then she thought about the manual Walter had given her on the plane and the detail it gave for handling dangerous situations. *Did he remember the protocol?* she wondered. *If he was arrested, did he remember that he was supposed to ask what the charges were and to call for immediate legal aid?*

"Did you try calling the jails?" Bev asked, with the revelation that if he had used his call to reach out to an attorney, he may not have been able to call Walter to let him know that he had been arrested.

"I did," Walter said, effectively dashing Bev's hopes. "I tried the Birmingham and Selma jails, and no one has any record of him."

"So what then? What do we do now?" The tears were starting to fall from Bev's eyes. She wasn't sure, though, whether she was crying because there was a possibility that another civil rights worker had been apprehended and tortured—maybe even killed—by racist vigilantes, or because she had deeper feelings for George. She had only known him for a couple of days, but the way he made her feel was undeniable. George was able to take Bev's mind off David in a way that she hadn't previously thought possible. When she left New York she wasn't sure if she could ever recover from David's rejection. Now she was actually looking forward to going out on a date with another man.

"There's nothing we can do, really," Walter answered. "I have a couple of federal connections who owe me some favors. I think it's still too early for me to reach out to them at this point, but if I haven't heard anything in a couple of days, I'll see if they can launch an investigation or at least be willing to force local authorities to do so."

"So we have to wait before we can even do anything? Anything could happen to him out there!" Bev yelled. "That's just not good enough!"

"You're absolutely right, Beverly," Walter said. "But that's all we have right now."

Leroy brought over three plates with turkey, lettuce, and tomato sandwiches and a side of potato salad. He set them on the table before saying, with little emotion, "Welcome to Alabama."

With George missing, Walter drove Bev and Mary into Perry County, were they had been assigned to make home visits. Bev had no idea what they would encounter, but it didn't take long to realize that Negroes in and around Marion, Alabama, didn't have "register to vote" at the top of their to-do lists.

The first house Bev and Mary visited was inhabited by Virgil Thomas. Virgil answered the door after the first knock with a small boy at his feet who, upon seeing Walter, Mary, and Bev, proceeded to run right back into the house.

"Y'all the police?" Virgil questioned as he took inventory of the three strangers on his front porch.

"No, sir," Mary said politely.

"Well, y'all must be lost, then," he said. "Ain't no white folks coming round these parts 'less they lost. Or the police."

"Mr. Thomas, we are volunteers with the Medical Committee for Human Rights, and we are working locally with the Student Nonviolent Coordinating Committee and the Southern Christian Leadership Conference to register Negro voters in your county," Walter explained. "May we come in and speak with you briefly?"

"Uh, I really don't think that's gon' be necessary, sir," Virgil said, slowly closing the door as he spoke. "I talked to some other folks like y'all a while ago. Told 'em I just ain't all that interested in registering right now."

"Can I ask why?" Walter said, stepping into the doorway just enough to keep it open.

Virgil sighed long and deep. "You heard of Jimmie Lee Jackson, the boy that got killed last month after protesting over by the jailhouse?"

"Of course. It's really unfortunate what happened to him."

"Well, he grew up not too far from here. Knew his folks real well. And Jimmie Lee was a good kid. He just got too carried away with all the protestin' and demonstratin'. Can't no good come from that. You see what them white folks did to him, to his momma and his granddaddy."

Virgil shook his head from side to side in apparent grief and looked back into the house where the boy had disappeared. "My son ain't but seven years old, you understand? I got to make sure I'm around for him. His momma died when she gave birth to him, and I'm all he got left. I think he'd rather have me around than see somethin' bad happen on account of me angerin' them white folks for no reason."

"Actually, Mr. Thomas," Bev said as she slid her body in front of Walter's to talk to Virgil directly, "registering to vote isn't for *no reason*. If you register and become a part of the political process, you can have a direct impact on your son's future. I'd say that's a pretty nice gift you could give as his father."

Virgil was agitated by Bev's persistence. "Look. I appreciate y'all comin' by here. But I'm not interested, okay? Now, I got to go. Excuse me." And he slammed the door in their faces.

Walter quickly headed down the front steps of the porch to map out their next stop. "Let's see," he said, looking down at a stack of papers he was holding. "Pearl Watkins is five houses down. She should be home from work now, so maybe we should head there next."

"Excuse me," Bev said, still standing on Virgil's porch and looking quite upset. "You're not going to say anything to him?" She motioned toward the house behind her. "You're giving up too easily. He just doesn't understand how important this is! We need to explain it more thoroughly!"

"Beverly, come here now," Walter said firmly. He waited for Bev to pout her way down the steps and over to the curb where he stood with Mary before continuing. "I appreciate your eagerness, but it's not for you to say what Mr. Thomas does or doesn't understand. No matter why *we* believe he should register to vote, we cannot force him to, nor can we impress our beliefs on him. We will walk through his neighborhood today, and tomorrow we will be gone. We will not be here for any backlash or ramifications that he experiences because of his decision. Do you understand that?"

"Yes, sir," Bev said, quietly and clearly deflated.

"We will encourage everyone we speak with to register, and we will most certainly detail the benefits of doing so. But we will not impose, and we will certainly not judge or ridicule their opinions. Is that understood?"

Bev and Mary nodded their heads in unison and followed as Walter started walking toward Pearl Watkins's home. As they approached the curb in front of her house, the sound of screeching tires stopped them immediately.

"I had a feelin' I'd be seeing y'all again," Tommy shouted from the window of his patrol car. "You wanna tell me what y'all doing out here 'round all these niggers?"

Bev had the same feeling she did in the back of George's Bonneville. Her stomach dropped to her knees. Instinctively, she glanced up and down the street, looking for places to hide among the tiny homes in the event she needed to run. There was no way she was going to be subjected to the same humiliation she had been before. There was some relief, though, as she peered into Tommy's car and saw that the passenger seat was empty.

"Excuse me," Walter said firmly, "but aren't you outside of your jurisdiction?"

Tommy laughed, revealing the tobacco in his cheek. "Ain't you learned nothin' yet, boy? I can go wherever I want. You, on the other hand, oughta be *real* careful 'bout your steps." He gave the three of them an ugly sneer. "I heard what happened to the other fella that was with y'all. George, right? Such a shame, ain't it?"

"Do you know something? *Where is he?*" Bev demanded, suddenly unable to control herself. She had taken two steps toward the patrol car when Tommy pulled his pistol out of its holster on his belt and pointed it straight at Bev.

"Now you listen here, girl," Tommy snapped. "I don't know how things work in New York, but 'round here, we don't stand for no woman talking outta turn. You hear me?"

Bev stood silent, frozen in place while Walter eased his body in front of hers. "We're just visiting friends," Walter said. "There's no problem here."

Tommy hesitated before he put his gun down. Then he spat—directly in Walter's face. "This is my second warning," he said. "There won't be a third."

While Tommy drove away, Walter pulled a handkerchief from his pocket and wiped the brown slime from his nose.

"I'm sorry," Bev said. "I shouldn't have said anything."

"No, you shouldn't have," Walter replied flatly. "You shouldn't have said anything at all."

The next day, Bev was still reeling from the run-in with Tommy. She was suddenly unsure of her place in Selma, and despite trying to remind herself of the advice she'd given Mary, she secretly wondered if she should head back home. But in the meantime, she also knew there was still work to be done. They'd never made it to Pearl Watkins's home, since Walter decided that, after being spit on, they should just head back. So, the next day, her house was the first stop the three of them made.

Pearl lived with her five children, aged three to twelve, and her elderly mother. To earn a living, she ironed clothes for a white woman in town, earning $2.50 a day. To supplement her meager wages, she also had a small garden with a few potatoes and a couple of lettuces in the backyard.

As they stood in the entryway of Pearl's small home, Bev was reminded of the warning Walter have given her and Mary in the car on the ride from the airport in Birmingham to Selma. He had told them that the living conditions they'd experience would likely pale in comparison to what they were used to. And while they had been somewhat spoiled staying with Leroy and Essie Mae, the Watkins residence was a stark reminder of the reality that many Negroes faced.

There was running water at least, but there was no shower. And there was no washing machine or telephone. In fact, it seemed as though Pearl's home had been transported from at least a generation prior, as there was little to indicate that it was being occupied in 1965. But what Pearl lacked in modern convenience she more than made up for with her cleanliness and hospitality. The little house was spotless and immaculately kept. The faded yellow curtains on the windows looked carefully pressed, and Bev, Walter, and Mary hadn't been in her home more than sixty seconds before she was offering to make coffee.

"You don't have to, really," Bev pleaded.

"It's no problem," Pearl said. "I don't know how long y'all been walking, but I'm sure y'all could use some refreshments." She pulled a cracked ceramic platter with a half-eaten cake on it from the countertop. "I got some pound cake, too," she said, smiling. "I baked it for dinner last Sunday and had a few pieces left. I don't like the kids to eat too much sugar and Momma's got problems with her sugar already."

"I'd love a piece," Bev said, as Walter and Mary both echoed her sentiment. "And some coffee, too."

Bev watched as the petite, chocolate-colored woman flitted about the kitchen, pulling together a haphazard collection of mismatched cups and saucers. Bev was drawn to the obviously overworked woman, who was a gracious hostess, despite her limited means.

"So have you ever considered registering to vote?" Bev asked as Pearl placed the coffee and cake on the table in front of them.

"Um, not really. I mean, no, ma'am," Pearl said politely. "My husband used to talk about it sometimes, but nothing ever came of it. Now I just focus on work and taking care of my family."

"Where's your husband?" Bev asked, as Walter glared at her. "If you don't mind me asking, that is. I don't want to pry." She flashed a smile back at Walter.

"No, it's fine." Pearl's eyes glistened while she struggled to keep a polite smile on her face. "My husband, Percy, got picked up by police about five years ago. He was walking home from the corner store down the way one evening 'cause I had sent him out for some milk. Little Johnny, the neighbor's boy, came telling me that the police was yelling at Percy when he came out the store. Then they beat him till he fell to the ground, put cuffs on him, and shoved him in the back of the police car."

Bev watched as one solitary tear slid slowly down Pearl's cheek. "I'm sorry, y'all," Pearl said. "I don't mean to get so emotional. It's just I haven't seen Percy since he left for the store that day, and I haven't talked to him, either, since we don't have a phone."

"That's horrible!" Mary said in amazement.

"What was he charged with?" Bev asked, barely concealing her own shock. "Do you have any idea why he was arrested?"

"I don't. All I know is what Johnny told me. I don't even know if he got an attorney to help him. But I don't think he's had a trial or anything. I got a friend who mops floors down at the courthouse. She said she'd keep an eye out, see if she heard anything about Percy's case coming up. She ain't said anything about it yet."

"Well, that is just completely unacceptable, Mrs. Watkins," Bev said. "I can't imagine what life has been like since your husband has been gone."

"It's been tough, really." Pearl was dabbing at her eyes with a tattered handkerchief she pulled from the front pocket of her dress. "It ain't easy taking care of all these kids by myself. One day rolls into the next and I feel like I can't even keep my head above water." She looked up at Bev with reddened eyes. "I respect what y'all are trying to do, trying to get people registered and all. But if there's anything you can do about my husband, that would mean more to me than anything."

Bev looked at Walter with no idea how to respond. She was only in town for a couple of weeks at most, so she wasn't sure whether she could, or should, commit to helping Pearl seek legal aid for Percy. She was a social worker; how would she even begin? And she knew absolutely nothing about the judicial process in Selma, particularly for Negroes. It seemed like a no-win situation, and despite Bev's tremendous empathy for Pearl, she didn't see what she could possibly do to help her.

"Walter?" Bev said, with tears now starting to fall from her own eyes. "Surely there is someone you can call, isn't there? Just to check and see, get an update on his case or something? It's been *five years*."

"I'll see what I can do," Walter said. "I can't make any promises, but I will certainly see what I can do. And I am so sorry that you're going through this. These are the injustices that we are fighting every day, the wrongs within the system that we want to try and make right." He looked Pearl in the eyes. "May God bless you, Mrs. Watkins. No one should ever be put in a situation like this."

Bev was still crying when she walked out of Pearl's house with Walter and Mary. She felt trapped and hopeless, that she was wasting her time. How were they going to get any of these people to be willing to register to vote when their problems seemed so insurmountable and all-consuming? On a daily basis, they were struggling just to survive. Bev felt it almost insensitive to go into their homes and talk to them about anything other than helping them meet their basic needs. She had encountered some dire situations through her work in New York, but nothing had prepared her for the tragically unfair existence of Negroes in the South.

The three of them were walking back up the street to Walter's car when they noticed an elderly man sitting on his porch. He waved at them. "How ya'll doing this fine day?" he shouted. "Don't look like y'all from around here . . ."

"Hello, sir," Bev said as she turned to walk toward the house where the man was sitting, motioning to Walter and Mary to let them know she'd catch up with them in a bit. "We're volunteers, here to help Negroes register to vote. Are you registered, sir?"

"Yes, ma'am; proud to say I am." The man sat up straight in his rocking chair. "Me and my grandson got registered together last year." He smiled at the memory. "That boy wasn't afraid of rufflin' no feathers, that's for sure."

He narrowed his eyes and peered closely at Bev. "Say, you look familiar," he said. "Any chance you were in the march to Montgomery yesterday?"

"Actually, I was," Bev replied.

"I knew it. I never did forget no face. Not in all my eighty-two years. I'm Cager Lee," he said, extending his hand to shake Bev's. "How do you do?"

"Beverly Luther, and it's a pleasure to meet you," Bev said. "So you were at the march?" Secretly, Bev wondered how the old man could have managed the whole trip had they been successful in walking the fifty-plus miles to Montgomery.

"Yes indeedy. I was there for my grandson, the one I was just talking 'bout. See, all that rabble-rousing I mentioned ended up costing him his life not too long ago." Mr. Lee closed his eyes and leaned back in his chair again. "Umm-hmm. He was shot to death last month at a protest for another young fella who was in jail. Pastor Bevel and some other good folks decided to have a march in his honor and said I should come along, too. I said yes, but I was a little worried 'bout making it all the way—I ain't no spring chicken now, if you know what I mean."

Mr. Lee laughed, and Bev did, too. "So Jimmie Lee Jackson was your grandson?" she asked.

"Yes, ma'am." He nodded again. "I guess you *would* know 'bout him, what with all the TV reporters and newspapers. You know, they didn't have all that around when I was a boy. Only way you got the news was for somebody to come and tell you."

Bev glanced up the block and saw that Walter and Mary were standing in front of Walter's car, waiting. "I don't have long," she said, turning to face Mr. Lee, "but can you please tell me what it's like, to have lost your grandson like that?"

Mr. Lee shifted just enough in his chair to turn and look at Bev. The deep creases around his eyes told of a long, hard life and of seeing more injustice than any one man should in a lifetime.

"I was there that day, you know?" he said as he rocked slowly back and forth. "Only reason Jimmie Lee even got shot was 'cause them troopers was beatin' up on me and his momma. He stepped in tryin' to save us. It ain't never easy losing someone you love, but when they gone 'cause they tried to save you? Well, that just make it even harder."

"I'm so sorry," Bev said.

"Don't be; ain't no need. In the end, I can still respect what Jimmie Lee was tryin' to do. See, in my day, we knew wasn't much we could do 'bout white folks and how they treat us. Shoot, my momma and daddy was slaves, so we was lucky just to be able to come and go as we please. But this a different time now."

Mr. Lee closed his eyes and tilted his face up to the sun. "It's time for some things to change, and it's happenin' right now. It's gon' be hard, and we might lose some brave folks along the way, but it's all worth it in the end, you know? Can't be mad at nobody willing to die so somebody else can have a better life."

Bev smiled as the man opened his eyes and looked at her again. "And you, miss," he said. "Ain't gon' be easy for you, either. Some Negroes ain't gon' be too trustin' of white folks, and your own kind gon' turn they backs on you for even wanting to help. But you just hang in there and keep fightin' for what's right. If we gon' win, we all got to fight together."

Bev carried Mr. Lee's words in her heart for the rest of the day, and she did feel somewhat comforted by them. But by the time night descended upon the Simpson home and she crawled into bed next to a soundly sleeping Mary, any reassurance she'd previously felt had completely dissipated. After a few minutes of tossing and turning, Bev got up, threw her robe around her shoulders, and tiptoed to the living room. She sat at the kitchen table and reached up to grab the telephone receiver.

"Hello," Lolly said groggily, after five long rings.

"Hi, Mother. How are you?"

"Bev, honey!" Bev could hear her mother sit up in bed and turn on the small lamp on her nightstand. "What time is it?"

"It's 1:30 a.m. here in Selma, so it's 11:30 there."

"Oh my goodness," Lolly said. "I didn't realize it was so late. Is everything all right? Why are you calling at this hour?"

"I couldn't sleep." Bev paused, trying to think of a way to articulate everything she was feeling at that moment. "I've been here a while now, Mother, but I'm not sure if I should leave."

"Yes, it has been a while," Lolly agreed. "I was surprised that I didn't hear from you sooner. But tell me, now, why is it you want to leave? Isn't there going to be a third march?"

"Yes . . . there is . . . but so much has happened." Bev was hesitating.

"Sweetheart, I can't help if you don't talk to me."

"Okay . . . well, first, we got pulled over by a couple of highway patrolmen on the way to Selma from the Birmingham airport. And it was horrifying. We stood on the side of the highway while they harassed us and called us nigger lovers." She kept going before her mother could respond. "Then, after the march on Tuesday, a bunch of us were eating at a local Negro restaurant when a truck full of Klansmen rode up and attacked a white minister who had participated in the march. To make matters worse, the guy who took him to the hospital—the MCHR worker who picked us up from the airport—never made it back. He's been missing since Tuesday, and he could be any-where between here and Birmingham. Oh, and the same patrol-man that pulled us over pulled a gun on me when we were going door to door registering voters." Bev took a deep breath and wiped tears from her eyes. She knew she was overwhelmed, but just speaking everything out loud made it that much realer.

"Beverly, I'm so sorry. I'm so, so sorry. I just can't even imag-ine what you're going through."

Bev could hear her mother's muffled tears on the other end, and she suddenly felt bad for calling. She didn't want her mother to worry, even though the truth was that she had very real reasons to be concerned. "Don't cry, please," Bev said. "I'm fine. Just shaken up a bit, that's all."

"It's more than that, and I know it," Lolly said sternly. "And I don't want you to think you have to act tough to protect me. I am your mother. And you're not made of steel. It's okay to be hurt and scared sometimes."

"So you think I should go home?"

"That's not what I said. I said it's okay to feel how you feel. It's nothing to be ashamed of." Lolly paused. "Are you afraid that something's going to happen to you? Is that why you want to leave?"

"I don't know . . . I don't think so." Bev struggled to answer the same question she'd asked herself so many times already. "I guess I just wonder if it's all even worth it," she said finally. "I know the cause is great, but it seems like the progress is so slow. And so many people are getting hurt or killed in the process."

"Casualties of war . . ."

"I know, but how can we even be sure we're winning? Johnson could step in and stop this nonsense at any moment, but where is he?" Bev could feel tears welling up again. "And you should see some of the people we've met here, Mom. Such nice, gracious people, and they live in absolute squalor. I met a woman today who is trying to support seven people on $2.50 a day. A *day*. And she even offered us refreshments when we showed up at her house!" Bev took a deep breath and lowered her voice. "There are so many people who are entitled to government assistance, but they keep getting denied or turned away before they can even apply. The system is so broken, and voting rights are just the beginning of the mess."

Lolly sat quietly on the other end of the line before she responded. "Beverly, honey, you can't focus on the things that are outside of your control. The police, the president, those are things that you can't change, and being upset about them does no good. But if there is anything you *can* control, any way to help the people right now, today, you need to do it."

"I don't think I understand," Bev said, confused.

"It's not always about big marches and protests," Lolly explained. "I don't profess to know anything about the experiences of those people there, but I do know what it's like to be a young widow struggling to take care of her children. You and your sister were such a tremendous help to me, so I know you can find a way to help the people in Selma."

Bev leaned back in her chair and studied a small crack in the kitchen ceiling. Her mother was right. There was plenty she could do to help. "Thanks for talking, Mom," she said, with renewed vigor. "I'm going to stay."

"I knew you would."

"How?"

"Because you're a fighter, Bev. Sometimes fighters get knocked around a bit, but the good ones always get back up again."

TEN

It was déjà vu.

As Bev looked around at the hundreds of mourners, packed standing room only into the sanctuary of Brown Chapel, she was immediately taken back to that hot, sticky day the previous August when she and David said their final good-byes to Mickey Schwerner. The crowds at both services were similar—Negro and white, with a good smattering of journalists and high-ranking federal officers mixed in.

In fact, it was that last group of attendants who had the residents of Selma and nearby Marion so upset. Ever since Minister Reeb's wife, Marie, had decided to take him off life support the morning of Thursday, March 11, white folks all over the country had been up in arms over the racial violence that was taking place in Alabama. Thanks to the media's eagerness to report on Minister Reeb's attack and his untimely death that followed, even President Johnson and members of the US Congress were speaking up. But there were no cameras or reporters when Jimmie Lee Jackson was shot dead.

Bev shifted in her pew and mentally counted the distinguished white folks at Brown Chapel who wouldn't have even considered showing up for Jimmie Lee's funeral service. Like Mickey's death, the fatal beating of Minister Reeb seemed to galvanize people in a way that hadn't yet been possible. What was it, she wondered, that made the life of a white man so much more valuable and worthy of recognition than that of a Negro?

Marie Reeb was sitting in the front pew, with the same look of heartbreak and devastation that Rita had worn. Bev wondered how she, personally, would react in that situation, if the man she had promised to spend the rest of her life with were suddenly ripped away from her in an act of brutal rage. She wondered, too, whether their husbands' murders were that much harder for Rita and Marie to accept, considering the fact that the men they loved were all too eager to walk directly into the line of fire. In an interview with television reporters who were gathered outside the hospital the morning after Minister Reeb was admitted, Marie said her husband believed so strongly in the movement that almost nothing could have kept him from traveling to Selma—even though he was well aware of the incredible risks.

Bev thought of George. He was like Mickey and Minister Reeb in so many ways, with his passion for civil rights so tangible. And she sensed that, like Mickey and Minister Reeb, George would be willing to give his life to further the movement. She hoped he wouldn't have to, though, even as she did the quick math in her head and realized that today, March 15, marked the sixth day he had been missing.

On the third day after George disappeared, Walter had finally decided to reach out to his Washington contacts, with the assumption that had he been arrested, George would have likely tried to call by then. But since Walter's frequent attempts to call the jails had turned up nothing, the possibility that he'd been picked up by the Klan or some other angry mob was more real than ever. They could only hope to find him before he was killed, and with so many back roads and isolated wooded areas, there was no way they could find him without the help of authorities.

As the days wore on with no news on George's safety, Bev shifted between feelings of worry and utter despair. Certainly, she would have been concerned had anyone she knew gone missing. The fact was, working with the civil rights movement placed enormous targets on the backs of everyone involved. Bev understood that and admired the courage of people like George

who knew and accepted the risks completely, and she was justi-
fiably grief-stricken when their bravery resulted in their own
harm or—in the worst cases—death.

Even still, Bev wasn't sure how she was supposed to feel
about George. She'd felt an undeniable attraction to him, and
the more they talked, the more she felt drawn to him. Finally, as
they danced in the corner of the Sweet Spot before Minister
Reeb was attacked, Bev was starting to believe that having a real
relationship with George, far away from the racially charged atmosphere of Selma, wasn't so far-fetched.

But Bev knew that didn't give her a right to feel the way
Marie and Rita did. George wasn't her husband. If she never
saw him alive again, he would just be some man she'd known
for a few days.

And if he should die,
Take his body, and cut it into little stars.
He will make the face of heaven so fine
That all the world will be in love with night.

Bev turned her attention to the Brown Chapel pulpit as Dr. King
stood at the microphone. She had long studied his grace and
elegance, and now he was quoting Shakespeare. She smiled to
herself as he continued.

"These beautiful words from *Romeo and Juliet* so eloquently describe the radiant life of James Reeb," Dr. King said. "He entered the stage of history just thirty-eight years ago, and in the brief years that he was privileged to act on this mortal stage, he played his part exceedingly well."

Already the choruses of "Amen!" and "All right!" were swelling in the sanctuary. But Dr. King was just getting started, just beginning to launch into that oratorical greatness that revered him to so many.

"The world is aroused over the murder of James Reeb, for he symbolizes the forces of goodwill in our nation," Dr. King said. "He demonstrated the conscience of the nation, and he was an attorney for the defense of the innocent in the court of world opinion. He was a witness to the truth that men of different races and classes might live, eat, and work together as brothers."

Bev looked up and saw Marie Reeb dab at the corners of her eyes with a handkerchief just in time to feel tears stinging the backs of her eyes as she thought of George again. *Why must good men die for doing good?*

Bev could see several reporters around the room furiously scribbling into notepads. And, again, she had that sensation that she was a part of history in the making. She was just a bit player in the monumental drama, sure, but she was in the production nonetheless.

"James Reeb was murdered by the indifference of every

minister of the gospel who has remained silent behind the safe security of stained glass windows. He was murdered by the irrelevancy of a church that will stand amid social evil and serve as a taillight rather than a headlight, an echo rather than a voice."

There were goose bumps on Bev's arms as Dr. King went on to add politicians, law enforcement, the federal government, and even "the cowardice of every Negro who tacitly accepts the evil system of segregation, who stands on the sidelines in the midst of a mighty struggle for justice" to his indictment. For what had been written off as a battle between southern Negroes and the white, segregationist thugs who struggled to keep them in their "place," King had implicated every single man and woman in America. And she realized, then, that Leroy was right. Dr. King knew exactly what he was doing. In turning around on that bridge to Montgomery, Dr. King was in no way acquiescing to the demands of Jim Clark and his savage army. He was, instead, using his calm confidence to call attention to the hatred that killed Minister Reeb and Jimmie Lee and Mickey—the same hatred that now had George clutched in its mighty grip. And in the process, he was daring everyone else who watched in horror to speak up on behalf of the oppressed, lest they be considered just as guilty as the oppressor.

"So in his death, James Reeb says something to each of us, black and white alike," Dr. King continued. "He says that we must substitute courage for caution; he says to us that we must be concerned not merely about who murdered him, but about the system, the way of life, the philosophy which produced the murder. His death says to us that we must work passionately— unrelentingly—to make the American dream a reality, so he did not die in vain."

What started out merely as a speech to honor one of the movement's most dedicated soldiers morphed quickly into a revival of sorts. For all those whose lights had been dimmed, even slightly, from the unresolved murders and the crooked cops and the general frustration that comes from fighting a seemingly winless fight, there was a reawakening in that church. Bev felt it within herself, too. She felt different—better, even—after spending a week with these people who were bold enough to keep getting up when, generation after generation, they had been knocked flat onto their backs.

Bev stood with everyone else as Dr. King's voice lifted above the heads of the men and women gathered there and floated right out the doors of Brown Chapel, down the streets of Selma and up and across every highway and byway in America.

"Look to me like any time we wanna get them folks in Washington to do their jobs, a white boy gotta die first," Leroy said.

After the service at Brown Chapel, Bev hitched a ride with

Walter and headed back to Leroy and Essie Mae's. She spoke briefly to Mary, who had decided not to go to the funeral because of a lingering migraine, and collapsed on one of the sofas in the living room. She was making her way through the first pages of Richard Wright's *Native Son* when she must have dozed off. "What are you talking about?" she asked Leroy, still groggy from her sleep.

"This," Leroy said, waving a finger at the black-and-white television set across the room. "President Johnson fixin' to make a statement 'bout all the craziness goin' on down here. As if it ain't been goin' on before that white boy got beat." Bev could hear the anger in his voice. "I tell you what, don't nothin' get folks attention like a dead white man—especially if they think he wasn't 'posed to die."

Bev sat up in the chair and stretched her legs out in front of her as she stared at the screen. Finally, the president appeared. He was standing in the House chamber of the US Capitol, preparing to address a slew of similarly dressed white men in dark suits. "Turn that up," she said to Leroy. "I want to hear this."

"'Course you do," he replied. "Let's see how he gon' talk his way outta this mess."

Bev was legitimately curious to hear how Johnson would publicly respond to Reeb's attack. On a private note, while the minister lay near death in a bed at the University of Alabama at

Birmingham Hospital, the president called Marie to offer his support, as well as use of Air Force One to fly to Alabama to be with her husband. It was a strong move for a man who, as George and many others believed, had done relatively little to support the ongoing civil rights efforts in the South.

When Dr. King was arrested and thrown in jail following a February 4 march in Selma that violated a citywide antiparade ordinance, he spent his days writing "Letter from a Selma Jail," which was later published in the *New York Times*. It was only then that Johnson agreed to address the lack of voting rights among Negroes. On the sixth of February the president announced that he would send a proposal to Congress, but he never stated when, specifically, he would introduce legislation. Hopefully, he would address it now.

"I speak tonight for the dignity of man and the destiny of democracy," Johnson began. "I urge every member of both parties, Americans of all religions and of all colors, from every section of this country, to join me in that cause."

"'Bout time," Leroy muttered under his breath.

"At times, history and fate meet at a single time in a single place to shape a turning point in man's unending search for freedom," Johnson continued. "So it was at Lexington and Concord. So it was a century ago at Appomattox. So it was last week in Selma, Alabama.

"There, long-suffering men and women peacefully protested the denial of their rights as Americans. Many were brutally assaulted. One good man, a man of God, was killed.

"There is no cause for pride in what has happened in Selma. There is no cause for self-satisfaction in the long denial of equal rights of millions of Americans. But there is cause for hope and for faith in our democracy in what is happening here tonight. Our mission is at once the oldest and the most basic of this country: to right wrong, to do justice, to serve man."

Bev sat up a little straighter on the sofa, eager to hear the president's plan to right the wrongs that were too numerous to count.

"There is no Negro problem. There is no southern problem. There is no northern problem," Johnson said. "There is only an American problem. And we are met here tonight as Americans—not as Democrats or Republicans. We are met here as Americans to solve that problem.

"This was the first nation in the history of the world to be founded with a purpose. The great phrases of that purpose still sound in every American heart, North and South: All men are created equal. Government by consent of the governed. Give me liberty or give me death. Well, those are not just clever words or empty theories. Those words are a promise to every citizen that he shall share in the dignity of man. This dignity cannot be found in a man's possessions; it cannot be found in his power or in his position. It really rests on his right to be treated as a man equal in opportunity to all others. It says that he shall share in freedom; he shall choose his leaders, educate his children, and provide for his family according to his ability and his merits as a human being. To apply any other test—to deny a man his hopes because of his color or race, his religion or the place of his birth—is not only to do injustice, but it is to deny America and to dishonor the dead who gave their lives for American freedom."

Bev stared slack-jawed at the TV. Lyndon Johnson had never been known for his oratorical skills. In fact, his thick Texas accent often made him difficult to understand in recorded speeches. But here, he wasn't just doing an okay job, he was making a truly compelling argument to the men he stood before and to all the people across the United States. How could any of them call themselves Americans, in the truest sense of the word, and not support the rights and liberties of their fellow Americans? His delivery was strong and direct, yet it played to the rational sensibilities of everyone who had tried to dismiss "the Negro problem" as something that didn't concern them.

"Our fathers believed that if this noble view of the rights of man was to flourish, it must be rooted in democracy," Johnson said. "The most basic right of all was the right to choose your own leaders. The history of this country, in large measure, is the history of the expansion of that right to all of our people.

"Many of the issues of civil rights are very complex and

most difficult. But about this there can and should be no argument. Every American citizen must have an equal right to vote. There is no reason which can excuse the denial of that right. There is no duty which weighs more heavily on us than the duty we have to ensure that right, yet the harsh fact is that in many places in this country men and women are kept from voting simply because they are Negroes."

Leroy jumped from his seat in the armchair adjacent to the sofa where Bev was sitting and clapped his hands. "Essie Mae, get in here!" he yelled toward the back of the house. "You gotta hear this!"

A few seconds later, Essie Mae emerged from their bedroom, smelling like patchouli and carrying two knitting needles and what looked like the beginning of a quilt. "What is it, baby?" she asked.

"Johnson!" Leroy said, again waving wildly in the direction of the TV. "He's on here talking 'bout how everybody in America—even Negroes—*must* be given their right to vote. Ain't no other way around it, he said."

"Wow, I can't believe it," Essie Mae said as she sat down next to Bev. "Looks like things are finally changing, huh?" Bev smiled at her before they all returned their attention to the president.

"Every device of which human ingenuity is capable has been used to deny this right," he said. "The Negro citizen may go to register only to be told that the day is wrong, or the hour is late or the official in charge is absent. And if he persists, and if he manages to present himself to the registrar, he may be disqualified because he did not spell out his middle name or because he abbreviated a word on the application. And if he manages to fill out an application he is given a test. The registrar is the sole judge of whether he passes this test. He may be asked to recite the entire Constitution, or explain the most complex provisions of state law. And even a college degree cannot be used to prove that he can read and write—for the fact is that the only way to pass these barriers is to show a white skin."

"Ha! You hear that?" Leroy could barely contain his excitement and was nearly jumping up and down. "Sound like ol' man Johnson musta visited some of these polls right here in Selma!"

Essie Mae shook her head. "Will you hush and sit down so we can hear what the man got to say?"

Johnson kept talking. "Experience has clearly shown that the existing process of law cannot overcome systematic and ingenious discrimination. No law that we now have on the books—and I have helped to put three of them there—can ensure the right to vote when local officials are determined to deny it.

"In such a case our duty must be clear to all of us. The Constitution says that no person shall be kept from voting because of his race or his color. We have all sworn an oath before God to support and to defend that Constitution. We must now act in obedience to that oath."

This was it, Bev thought. The moment that would change the course of history as they all knew it. It would begin to rectify the deaths of James Reeb and Mickey Schwerner, and it would mean that their wives weren't going to bed alone each night in vain.

"Wednesday I will send to Congress a law designed to eliminate illegal barriers to the right to vote," Johnson said emphatically, as his eyes scanned the men sitting around the room. "The broad principles of that bill will be in the hands of the Democratic and Republican leaders tomorrow. After they have reviewed it, it will come here formally as a bill. And this bill will strike down restrictions to voting in all elections—federal, state, and local—which have been used to deny Negroes the right to vote."

Then, to put an end to any remaining doubt that the tide had finally shifted in favor of the disenfranchised Negro, he added, "To those who seek to avoid action by their national government in their own communities, who want to—and who seek to—maintain purely local control over elections, the answer is simple: Open your polling places to all your people. Allow men and women to register and vote whatever the color of their skin. Extend the rights of citizenship to every citizen of this land."

No ambiguity, no uncertainty. The president drew his line in the sand and made it very clear which side he was standing on. And he urged the members of Congress to join him, to do what was necessary to pass the bill. No one was naive enough to believe that it would happen overnight, but this step was huge, and it served notice to any hooded Klansmen or badge-wearing sheriffs who thought they could continue to isolate the Negro people and beat them into submission. Now, they had the federal government of the most powerful country in the world on their side.

"But even if we pass this bill, the battle will not be over," Johnson said, as if hearing Bev's thoughts. "What happened in Selma is part of a far larger movement which reaches into every section and state of America. It is the effort of American Negroes to secure for themselves the full blessings of American life.

"Their cause must be our cause, too, because it is not just Negroes, but really, it is all of us, who must overcome the crippling legacy of bigotry and injustice. And we shall overcome.

"As a man whose roots go deeply into southern soil I know how agonizing racial feelings are. I know how difficult it is to reshape the attitudes and the structure of our society. But a century has passed, more than a hundred years, since the Negro was freed. And he is not fully free tonight."

At the conclusion of the president's speech, Leroy hurried

over to the coat rack and grabbed his hat from the top. "Where are you going this late?" Essie Mae asked.

"To open the Sweet Spot," Leroy said in a rush. "We gotta celebrate!" Then he looked at Bev. "Are you gonna come by?"

"I wouldn't miss it," she replied. "This is definitely reason to celebrate."

ELEVEN

"WHAT'S YOUR NAME again?" the plump, bouffant-haired woman behind the desk asked. Her tone was short and snappy to match her irritated glare.

"Sarah Toombs. Mrs. Sarah Toombs."

Bev reached her hand up to Sarah's back and made small circles with her fingers on top of the silk blouse Sarah was wearing, trying to ease her anxiety. She could see tiny beads of sweat forming on her brown skin.

"And what is the problem?" the woman asked.

"Well, ma'am . . ." Sarah started. "I believe I'm entitled to Social Security benefits . . . You see . . . umm . . ."

Bev couldn't take it any longer. She and Sarah had been in the Dallas County Courthouse for over three hours, getting shuffled from one department to another. It was a miracle that she was even able to convince Sarah to go with her and demand the benefits that she should have been receiving for the past six years. Now she could tell Sarah was feeling intimidated and frustrated, and it wouldn't be long before she turned around and walked right back out the door, empty-handed.

"Look," Bev said to the clerk, matching her angry disposition. "Mrs. Toombs's husband died six years ago in an accident pouring concrete on a stretch of highway just outside of town. She, meanwhile, has been unable to work because she is caring for their children, the youngest of whom was born disabled." Bev looked at Sarah and nodded, confirming that, as promised, Bev would have everything under control.

When she had first arrived at Sarah's house the day before, Bev was intending, as usual, to try to convince Sarah to register to vote. And as usual, she discovered that Sarah had far greater concerns to deal with.

Sarah's five-year-old daughter, Elizabeth, was born with cerebral palsy just three months after Sarah's husband died. The umbilical cord was wrapped around her neck, and after she was born, the doctors at Burwell declared that she wasn't likely to survive. Little Elizabeth was a fighter, and she lived, but the damage to her brain from lack of oxygen was significant. She couldn't talk, so she communicated via a series of varied grunting noises, and while her arms functioned normally, her legs could barely support the weight of her body.

At the time of Elizabeth's birth, Sarah already had two other children to care for, aged two and three and a half, so dealing with Elizabeth's medical concerns only exacerbated the young mother's stress. Additionally, Sarah soon discovered that caring for Elizabeth was incredibly expensive, what with purchasing a wheelchair and leg braces and the regular doctor appointments. Elizabeth's frequent seizures meant that she needed around-the-clock care, making it impossible for Sarah to work outside the home.

When Bev heard the details of Sarah's story and learned that she had no family nearby to offer support—financial or otherwise—once her husband died, she immediately asked Sarah about her Social Security benefits. Her children would all be eligible for compensation, Bev assumed, and Elizabeth may have qualified for additional compensation because of her condition.

Sarah was a proud woman who had been forced to subsist on the meager wages she earned from selling cakes and pies out of her kitchen, plus any gifts from neighbors or church friends. Sarah called the occasional bags of groceries or money to pay her electric bill "gifts" because she couldn't bear the thought of being reduced to needing handouts. She wasn't opposed to government assistance, though, because she had heard it would come in the children's names. She felt justified, then, because that would mean she could buy the kids more than one pair of shoes a year and buy a new wheelchair for Elizabeth that actually had working wheels.

But Sarah's first—and only—attempt at securing benefits had failed miserably. She'd gone down to the courthouse only to be accosted and turned away by white police officers who laughed and told her to "find some other nigger to marry" who could help her take care of her kids.

That was four years ago. So when Bev promised to handle everything and secure financial benefits for her family, Sarah was both hesitant to endure more hatred and doubtful that it would even work. But Bev was persistent, stating confidently that she wouldn't leave Selma until Sarah and her children were taken care of. And she meant every word.

The courthouse clerk got up from her seat and waddled to a row of file cabinets behind her. She opened one drawer and proceeded to look through the files for all of fifteen seconds before returning to face them. "I am so sorry, but I don't have any record of your husband's death, or of the births of your children. There's nothing I can do." She plastered a smile on her face that was as fake as the bouquet of plastic flowers sitting on her desk.

Bev reached into the tote bag she carried on her arm, pulled out a stack of papers, and slammed them on the desk. "Here," she snapped. "Birth certificates for Gary Junior, John, and Elizabeth Toombs, and a death certificate for Gary Toombs Senior."

The woman studied Bev, trying to figure out the tiny woman who wasn't backing down. "I see . . . and who are you, miss?"

"Beverly Luther," Bev replied. "I am a friend of Mrs. Toombs, and I am here to make sure she gets what is rightfully hers."

"Ah, I see," the woman said with a smirk. "You're one of them nigger-loving Yankees down here agitating and stirring up trouble." She stood up and leaned across the top of the desk. "I'll tell you now, we won't be having any of that around here."

"The only trouble you're going to have, ma'am, is that of the federal government should you choose not to abide by the laws of the land," Bev said. "The guidelines are very clear, and they indicate that Mrs. Toombs's children are most certainly entitled to survivor benefits under the current Social Security legislation.

"Well, how 'bout I call a couple of police officers up here and tell them what's goin' on? You think this nigger bitch gon' get anything then?"

The clerk was cocky with her arms crossed in front of her, as if she knew Bev would back down after a police threat. But Bev didn't flinch. "Now, you may not have heard, but President Johnson has made it very clear that he will no longer tolerate any local government agencies who continue to deny Negroes their full rights under the law. He was speaking of voters' rights, specifically, but I'm sure he would agree that those inalienable rights should extend to the care of a widow with no way to support herself and her three children."

Satisfied, Bev stepped back and waited for the clerk to respond.

"Hmph," the woman grumbled. "I'll have to talk to my boss. . . ."

"Take your time," Bev replied with a smile. "We'll be right here waiting."

Forty-five minutes later, Bev and Sarah were standing in front of the courthouse with official documentation from Sarah's visit that stated she would be receiving her first check within three to four weeks.

For Bev, the victory at the Dallas County Courthouse was a turning point. Finally, she didn't feel that she was just an anonymous white face in a sea of brown. She had marched and gone door-to-door, yes. But to a certain degree, those were positions anyone could fill. What she had just done was proof that she, specifically, was an integral part of the movement.

It had taken some time, but seeing the civil rights struggle up close showed Bev that the battle wasn't just about segregated restaurants and water fountains. Those were the easy issues to heal. It was the poverty and limited access to quality education and health care that needed to be addressed. Those were the deeper wounds that would leave generational scars, and because of her extensive experience caring for at-risk populations in New York, Bev knew she was uniquely qualified to attend to the poor and vulnerable in Alabama.

"I don't know how to thank you," Sarah said as she threw her arms around Bev's shoulders. "This has been a long, long time coming. You have no idea what it's like to look your babies in the face and know you can't take care of 'em like you want to."

"You're right. I don't," Bev said. "But now you won't have to go through that again, either." She stuck her hand into her purse and pulled out a pen and a torn piece of paper. "This is my phone number back in New York," she said, scribbling the digits onto the paper. "If anything—and I mean *anything*—goes wrong, you call me. If a month has passed and you haven't gotten your check, you call me. And if you just need someone to talk to, you call me for that, too."

Sarah hugged Bev one last time. "You're my angel," she said.

The following day, on March 17, the voting rights bill was introduced to the Senate by Democrat Mike Mansfield, the Senate majority leader, and Everett Dirksen, the Senate minority leader. Dirksen was a Republican enlisted by President Johnson to rally the support of his party, in the event southern Democrats decided to filibuster the legislation and delay—or completely prevent—its passage. Dirksen supported the Civil Rights Act of 1964, and he hadn't initially intended to support any voting rights legislation so soon afterward. But seeing the brutality enacted against the protestors in the first Selma-Montgomery march changed his mind.

On the eighteenth, Bev, Mary, and about fifty other workers gathered in the multipurpose room in Selma's Negro Community Center to plan the third and final march, which had finally been scheduled to begin on Sunday, March 21.

"Are there any new orders of business?" asked Harry Boyte. He was a twenty-year-old white kid from North Carolina who had joined the SCLC in 1963 as one of Dr. King's assistants.

"Okay, then," Boyte said when no one spoke up. "The march starts Sunday, so we will be screening participants this coming Saturday, beginning at nine a.m. As you know, the federal injunction against marching has been lifted, so we will be continuing through to Montgomery, walking an average of twelve miles a day. We estimate that we will arrive at the Capitol on the twenty-fifth." Boyte paused briefly and scanned the crowd to see whether anyone had any questions before he continued. "At this time, Governor Wallace has refused to activate the Alabama National Guard on our behalf, so President Johnson has taken over and ordered the federal guard, along with FBI agents, to protect us on the journey."

There were a few shouts and claps before Boyte raised his hand to silence everyone. "Listen, this is certainly a win in our favor," he said, "but there is still much work to be done." Then, his tone grew serious, as if he were about to let the people in on a deep, dark secret. "During the march, part of Highway Eighty will narrow from four lanes to two. For safety reasons, only three hundred marchers will be allowed to continue. So it will be up to us to screen the marchers and select those three hundred."

Bev thought about the difficulty of the process, and how disappointed some of the thousands of hopefuls would likely be when they weren't chosen.

"On another note," Boyte continued. "I know many of you have been making home visitations here in Selma, as well as in Perry County. Would anyone like to report on the success of those outings?"

Bev immediately raised her hand and stood to her feet. "I will be quite honest, Mr. Boyte," she said. "It has been incredibly difficult to convince people to register to vote. I thought fear and intimidation would be the primary factors—and they are important—but I think people simply don't want to deal with that opposition when they have more pressing concerns."

"Concerns like what?" Boyte asked.

"The people are hungry, sir," Bev replied. "They earn very little money, so they are forced to subsist on scraps. I've met so many families who qualify for and should be receiving government assistance, but they haven't gotten one check. Also, here in Selma, there are no sidewalks in the Negro communities and some of the people live in areas where the sewage is so bad, you can smell it from miles away."

Bev saw many of the other volunteers nodding in agreement, acknowledging that they had encountered the same problems. She overheard a woman from Philadelphia comment that she had never seen such deprivation before.

"Here's how I see it," Boyte said, interrupting the side chatter. "Mr. Smitherton, the mayor of Selma, is responsible for his flock—the citizens of Selma. However, he doesn't seem to be very involved, at this point, with his Negro citizens. That they are living in such terrible conditions and that they have been brutalized by city and state police is unacceptable."

More affirmation rose from the crowd.

"So if Mayor Smitherton, who is a very great and important man, isn't going to come out and talk to the citizens of Selma about the injustices that are going on," Boyte continued, "then maybe we'll just have to go visit him at his home." He paused for effect. "I believe he lives at 603 Sixth Avenue in a beautiful white house. I'm sure there are many sightseers who would like to visit the mayor and see where he lives."

Bev was surprised that Boyte would so freely announce the mayor's address, but she also knew the level of organization and structure that existed within the movement. According to established protocol, the SCLC leadership would hand-select a group of volunteers, who would then designate a specific date and time to picket the mayor's home.

"So how have you been handling these difficulties?" Boyte asked, addressing Bev directly.

"Well, I didn't do much at first," Bev said. "I think I was too overwhelmed because the problem seemed too big. But then I just started thinking about my skills and what I know I can do to fix some of the problems, and I started acting on that." Boyte was smiling widely to indicate his approval, so Bev kept going. "A couple of days ago, I drove a woman down to the courthouse to see about her Social Security benefits. Everyone was giving us the runaround in the beginning, but I spoke on her behalf and got everything handled."

Boyte clapped his hands, and soon everyone else joined in the applause. "Wonderful!" he said, eyeing the seated workers. "This is the kind of real change that we need to make happen every day. There are a lot of injustices in this world, and right here in Selma, Alabama, too, but we mustn't focus on the mountains ahead and become too afraid to take even one step forward." Then he turned back to Bev. "We'll definitely need your intuition and initiative during the screenings."

Boyte's tone grew more serious as he addressed the crowd. "We've lost a lot of support from SNCC leaders and others who don't feel that the movement is effective enough on its own," Boyte continued. "Some folks think the only way we can be recognized is if a white person is killed." Bev sat silently and thought back to her conversation with Leroy and the frustration he felt. He'd heard of scores of Negro men killed before Minister Reeb, and there was little or no acknowledgment from anyone outside their local communities.

"But can you blame them?" Boyte said. "Can we honestly say that we've done everything we can?" He looked around at the faces before him again.

"It's true that the president of the United States sent flowers to James Reeb when he lay dying for five days in the hospital," Boyte said. "But when Jimmie Lee—who had been shot in the belly as he leaned over to protect his mother from the blows of the troopers—lay dying from stomach wounds in the hospital, the president sent no flowers.

"And do you know what else? There was a memorial fund set up by white America for Reverend Reeb," Boyte added, almost shouting. "But where is the memorial fund for Jimmie Lee?" Boyte scanned the white faces in the crowd, faces that looked like his, and like Bev's, and he said, "*You*, white America, *you* need to set up a fund for Jimmy Lee Jackson, too."

Bev felt a pang of guilt pierce her heart. It was so easy to think that because she made the commitment to take weeks off work and spend her own money to travel to Selma, she was doing all she possibly could to further the civil rights movement and improve the quality of life for Negroes in America. She marched and walked door-to-door on behalf of the Negro right to vote. And she was even willing to confront the white establishment to fight injustice toward men and women whom she barely knew.

But what if, *what if*, there was still more? What if Boyte was right and she was somehow taking the easy way out, only doing enough to pacify her own do-good intentions, but not enough to have a real impact? The thought frightened her.

Suddenly, loud noises were heard outside the community center. There were yells and screams coming from what sounded like an army of men.

"Everyone stay calm and move away from the windows," Boyte said, quickly taking action. He jumped off the podium and rushed to the multipurpose room's door, where he exchanged whispers with another SCLC leader. Moments later, they left the room. Bev stood near the door and watched the two men as they walked down the hallway and toward the entrance of the community center. Like Boyte, the other man was in his twenties, and with their boyish faces and thin builds, Bev wondered whether they could protect all the volunteers from whatever was raging outside.

After a few minutes, Bev heard Boyte speaking with another man who was just out of her view.

"Y'all ain't under arrest yet," the man said, "but for your own safety, I suggest y'all leave now, while I can protect you. There's about fifty men out there who ain't happy with all the marchin' and carryin' on y'all been doing."

"Excuse me, Mr. Baker, sir, but we're not doing anything unlawful here," Boyte responded. "I'm not sure why we need to leave."

"Look, I am the public safety director of Selma, and it is my job to protect your safety." Baker's voice dropped a couple of levels, so Bev had to strain to hear him. "Between me and you, I don't a hundred percent agree with the way Clark has been handling you boys, that's why I got several officers outside who will see you safely to your residences," he said. "But take my word, you are in great danger if you stay here."

Bev could hear bottles smashing against the walls outside along with a dog that was growling with ferocious intensity. She glanced back at the others, all clustered near the center of the room. She saw faces of worry—belonging mostly to white northerners—and she wondered how quickly everyone could gather their things once they were told it was okay to leave.

"One moment while I talk to my colleagues," Bev heard Boyte say. Then he and the other man moved back down the hallway in Bev's direction. Bev assumed her position near the door again, though she had no idea what they could possibly be talking about. Baker had already warned them not to stay.

"Do you think we should leave?" the man asked.

"I don't think so," Boyte said confidently. "We can't even be certain that Baker will protect us like he's saying. And what kind of message does that send, that we'll jump just because the Klan said to?"

"I know, Harry, but we've got women in there. We don't know what those fools out there are going to do."

"If you want to leave, you should leave," Boyte responded. "But the movement demands you stay."

Bev heard footsteps against the linoleum floor as they walked back to give Baker their decision.

"We're staying, sir, but thank you for your offer," Boyte said. "We understand the risks that await, but we are committed to the work that remains."

"Suit yourself," said Baker roughly. "I'm pulling away all police right now. Best of luck to you."

The door to the community center slammed shut, and within moments Boyte and the other man were back in the multipurpose room. Boyte walked back to the podium to address the crowd.

"Here's the deal," he said. "There's a mob of about twenty-five Klansmen outside who are quite upset about the work we've been doing to try to register voters."

There were whispers and mumbles making their way through the group, as everyone was anxious to hear next steps.

Boyte continued. "I just spoke with Wilson Baker, the public safety director of Selma, and while he promised to provide us with police escorts back to the homes where we're staying, Stephen and I think it's best if we take our chances in here."

With that, the crowd erupted. "Take our chances?!" shouted a middle-aged white woman from Chicago. "If we were promised safety, we should be leaving now! Who's going to protect us if they decide to come busting through the door?"

"You didn't have a right to make that decision without talking to us first," said another white volunteer. "We should each have a voice in this—it's our lives on the line."

Bev could see Stephen standing off to the side of the podium, his head down. She knew he didn't support Boyte's decision, and honestly, she didn't know whether it was the right choice either. But at that point, there was nothing more to argue about. The decision was made.

"Listen!" Bev shouted over the noise. "Our work has made us a lot of enemies here—including those people outside the door. They are intent on destroying anything that threatens their supremacy and their way of life, and that includes us." The room grew silent, as all eyes focused on her. "There is no guarantee that Baker would really protect us, so if Mr. Boyte thinks we have better odds in here, we should listen. And no matter what, we need to stick together and not fight."

Boyte shot Bev a look of appreciation. "She's right," he said. "We saw what happened to James Reeb at the hands of men like this. In fact, his killers could be outside right now. I say we stand firm and cling to the principles of this movement the way we've been doing. They have no right to disrupt our peaceful meeting."

Slowly, everyone began nodding their heads in agreement. Then, a local Negro volunteer from Selma stood and prayed for their protection, and the entire atmosphere inside the community center changed. Worry and fear was replaced by peace and love.

Boyte and the other leaders started assigning tasks and giving orders. First up, the windows were immediately closed to prevent tear gas or bombs from being thrown in. And to accommodate smokers, cigarettes were only allowed during the first fifteen minutes of every hour. There were a dozen monitors appointed over subsets of the group to ensure that everyone stayed calm. And to address the toilets that had been clogged since the beginning of the meeting, several men were declared in-house plumbers, and they quickly cleaned them out.

Many within the movement were aware that rumors were circulating that the movement was full of immorality and perversion, and that events had a tendency to morph into sexual orgies. This wasn't the case, obviously, but to solidify the leadership's position on any questionable behavior, the men were ordered to sleep downstairs while the women made sleeping arrangements on the top floor of the building. "We're not going to give white Selma—or the world—the chance to say that we all slept in the community center and had some sort of party," Boyte explained.

Christine Adams, a white volunteer from Greenwich Village, New York, took issue immediately. "This is ridiculous," she snapped. "I am an adult, and I thought the men here were adults as well. I would expect that we could all bottle any urges without being separated and assigned cots like children."

Boyte wasn't having it. "Miss Adams," he said calmly but sternly, "this matter is simply not up for debate. The question of whether the people can control themselves is not the point. It is our reputation and the reputation of the entire movement that is on the line here. We simply will not allow room for assumptions."

"Well, I have dedicated my time to be here for the *movement*," Christine snapped. "I am just as important as any of you with your fancy titles, and I will not be talked to like a child."

At that point, every single person in the room had stopped moving, stopped talking—Bev was sure some of the people had even stopped breathing in anticipation of Boyte's next move. He eyed her carefully, as if surveying the worthiness of his opponent, and then said, loud enough that only Christine could hear, "We appreciate your commitment. But this movement is not about any individual. It's a collective effort, and if you are not willing to conform to the standards already in place, we respect your decision and wish you well. There is the door," he added, pointing.

Almost as if to punctuate Boyte's words, loud gunfire echoed from outside.

Bev saw Christine's eyes follow the direction of his finger, but everyone knew there was no way she could leave. Christine gave Boyte one last glare, turned on her heels, and huffed and puffed her way upstairs, her blond ponytail swinging wildly behind her.

Boyte's poised but powerful reaction was indicative of the

gentle force that underscored the entire movement. No matter what the situation—no matter how unfair or tragic, disappointing or life-threatening—the leadership never lost their cool. They moved and spoke with a composure that demanded respect and—more often than not—was able to calm the opposition's raging fury.

After Christine walked upstairs, Bev followed her to help her find extra blankets for everyone.

"Are you all right?" Bev asked while they sorted through boxes of tennis balls and ping-pong paddles in the storage closet.

"I'm fine." Christine was hurriedly pushing boxes aside without even checking their contents.

"I don't mean to impose," Bev said carefully, "but it seems to me that this is about more than where you're going to sleep tonight."

Christine stopped in midmotion and turned to face Bev. "Are you trying to accuse me of something?"

Bev raised her palms in surrender. "I'm not saying that at all," she said. "I just get the sense that something more is bothering you. Are you sure you're okay?"

Christine sighed. Then she found an extra-large box that was still taped and sat on it. "Have you noticed that all the leaders of the movement are men?"

It sounded as if Christine was thinking out loud and not really expecting Bev to answer, so she didn't.

"I honestly don't have a problem with authority," she continued, "but when I notice that authority is comprised only of males who seem to have an old-fashioned perspective and controlling influence over the women, I take offense."

Bev wasn't sure how to respond. Yes, the leadership was comprised solely of males. And, yes, they had a tendency to be controlling and overly assertive at times. But she had never focused on this, instead choosing to believe it was a necessary evil of a very efficient and effective movement. If there was no one to take charge and force action, how would anything ever be accomplished?

"I understand your point," Bev said, choosing her words carefully. "But I don't think anyone here has any malicious intent. I think Mr. Boyte was right—that this movement is bigger than any of the individuals involved. So I just think any hurt feelings or misconceptions are by-products of the movement's larger scope."

Christine smirked. "What's your deal? I saw your little speech down there. You must be sleeping with one of them, huh? You're the reason all the women have been banished to the attic?"

"Christine, I traveled here from New York because I wanted to be a part of history, not end up in some man's bed, but quite frankly, that's none of your business," Bev said. "It is clear that you are having trouble adjusting to the order and structure of the movement, and for that I am sorry. The high level of organization and regimen is not for everyone, I guess. But one day, years from now, I have a feeling you will look back on these moments and wish that you had saved your venom for the true enemy. And you will realize that they were all on the other side of the door."

Christine responded only with silence as she stood and walked out of the storage closet. Bev couldn't tell whether she was still upset, but it didn't matter. There was no place for her negativity within the movement, and whether Bev always agreed with leadership or not, she wouldn't stand by and watch someone on the inside create division.

As for the Klansmen outside, no one ever knew whether Baker had come back and forced them to leave or whether they knew that with all eyes on Selma, any attacks on the volunteers just wouldn't be worth it. But shortly after one in the morning, the gunshots and barking dog and shouts of "Nigger!" and "Nigger lover!" were suddenly gone. Or maybe the hooded men were just tired after a long night of harassment. Everyone inside the community center certainly was, and once the night grew quiet, they all fell fast asleep.

The next morning, Bev was the first one up. She made a pit stop in the bathroom before heading outside to smoke, and once she stepped out of the main entrance, she was amazed at what she saw.

In an oak tree that stood about twenty yards from the community center's front entrance, two male effigies were hanging from a low branch—one black, one white. And spray painted in white on the expansive lawn were the words "WE HATE NIGGERS AND NIGGER LOVERS." If that sight alone weren't enough, there was garbage everywhere—literal garbage, presumably trucked in from the city dump. Bev could barely stand the stench as she stepped over rotten chicken carcasses and disposable diapers.

Bev cried softly as she surveyed the damage. The hate was so palpable it seemed to hang thick in the air, even though the mob of men had long dispersed. She wanted to curse the cowards who had done this, to pick up the trash and dump it in their yards while they slept. But she thought of George's words, and Amelia Boynton's, and her mother's, and Dr. King's, and the words of every person involved in the civil rights movement who had called for love when they had only felt hate. In that moment, Bev was overwhelmed with fiery anger and rage, but if she had learned nothing else from the great men and women around her, she knew the power of peace under pressure.

Bev took one last look at the disheveled lawn; then she retrieved the large trash can from behind the community center and started cleaning it all up.

TWELVE

Twenty-four hours later, after an entire day spent barricaded inside the Negro Community Center and picking up months-old garbage with her bare hands, Bev was locked inside Leroy and Essie Mae's tiny bathroom, running bathwater so hot that it completely clouded the mirror above the sink and threatened to scald Bev's skin as she dipped her toe in. Once her entire foot adjusted to the heat, she brought her other leg over the side of the tub until she was standing shin-deep, then she slowly lowered herself to a seated position. Finally, she pressed her back hard against the porcelain and slid down until just her head was above the steaming water.

Bev was exhausted and every muscle in her body was aching, not just from the hours of cleaning, or the flimsy cot she'd slept on, or the fact that she had subsisted the previous day only on stale saltine crackers, a piece of chewing gum, and a single cigarette. But she was emotionally and mentally wrecked.

She was still committing to doing everything that she could do to help, as her mother suggested. But the terror of staring down a racist officer's gun still haunted her, especially when she slept.

Of course, it didn't help matters that there was still no update on George's whereabouts. There had been a glimmer of hope when Walter got a call from the local police about a civil rights volunteer who had been arrested and brought in, but it was only Jackson Mabry, a white Montgomery native who had driven into Selma to participate in the first two marches.

She was genuinely worried for his safety, but there was something more, too. And that made Bev feel like a silly schoolgirl, that even in the midst of such a pivotal moment in American history, even as her own life was threatened, she was thinking about a boy, fantasizing about what could be once she got back home to New York. She created imaginary dialogue in her mind, wondering what her roommates would think of him and what they would say the first time she invited him over for coffee or drinks.

She was sure that her mother would like him, though that didn't necessarily mean much, since she liked David, too. After meeting him during Christmas, Bev's mother made it a point to ask about him during every phone conversation. She wanted to know the important things, like how his career was going and how well they were managing in their efforts to grow Social Workers for Civil Rights Action. But she was just as interested in the mundane aspects of David's life, such as whether he preferred double- or single-breasted suits and how many sugars he took in his coffee. It was as if she was preparing a mental file on him so that, in the event he became her son-in-law, she'd already be well prepared.

Not that she'd have to worry about that. Bev had purposely avoided telling her mother the details of her argument with David. No need to go into detail about how David would never be a part of their family, or how ironic it was that, despite Bev's work in the movement to try to level the playing field for Negroes, she was the one being discriminated against—how, in this case, her white skin actually worked against her.

Bev lifted a leg out of the water and propped her heel up on the foot of the tub. She stared at her pale skin and wondered what it would look like against David's. How, in an alternate universe, their bodies would make a bold geometric pattern of contrasts as they lay intertwined in bed on a sleepy Sunday morning. And their babies. Would their skin be a closer match to hers or his, or would it fall somewhere in the middle, like the rich café au lait that Bev loved from the little French shop near her office?

She sighed and lowered her leg back into the water. When thoughts of David would creep into her mind, she cursed them, feeling like a tortured masochist who couldn't stop punishing herself with fantasies of what would never be. And, sadly, as much as Bev genuinely enjoyed George's company and found herself attracted to him, perhaps the main reason she needed him was to keep David from infiltrating her mind.

After washing up quickly, Bev dried off and threw on some flannel pajamas before walking across the hall into the bedroom where Mary was already sleeping. She slid under the covers and closed her eyes, hoping for a clear head as she drifted off to sleep.

Saturday morning, just one day before the scheduled march to Montgomery, Bev was having her regular breakfast of coffee and a cigarette when Leroy joined her in the kitchen.

"Heard y'all had a rough night the other night," he said, as he took four large potatoes from a bowl on the countertop and began peeling and chopping them.

"Yeah," Bev said. "Some crazy Klan members showed up at the community center where we were meeting and threatened to kill us. They stayed out there most of the night, and before they left they spray-painted the lawn and dumped trash every-where."

"What? No burning cross?"

Bev wasn't sure if Leroy was joking or serious.

"I'm kidding." Leroy laughed. "We're used to these crazy white boys actin' a fool. Ain't nothin' new. But I bet y'all was probably wishin' y'all had a little help," he said, motioning toward his gun with his left hand while he poured Crisco into a cast-iron skillet with his right.

Bev returned the laugh. "Actually, Wilson Baker was there in the beginning with police support. He said he would escort us out safely if we wanted to leave and head home."

"Please," Leroy said sarcastically. "These white folks round here can't be trusted. Word on the street is, Baker ain't happy with how Clark been treating Negroes. Said he doin' more harm than good anyway, 'cause every time he beats some old woman over the head or sprays a kid with tear gas, the newspapers catch hold of it and go tellin' the whole world. Have folks all the way in California sympathizin' with us and wantin' to come help.

"But still," he continued, as he transferred the potatoes to the hot grease and pressed them down in one even layer, "for a public safety officer, he ain't been doing a good job of keepin' the public safe."

"That's what the leadership thought," Bev said. "They figured we'd be better off taking our chances barricaded inside, as opposed to walking right into the angry mob. No one was sure whether Baker could really be trusted to help us, and we were well within our legal rights for peaceful assembly."

"That's right," Leroy said. Then he turned from the stove to face Bev. "So how you feelin'? Like you bit off a little more than you can chew? Bet you wasn't expectin' to be holed up in no worn-down community center for twenty-four hours, huh?"

Bev smiled. Leroy was right—she hadn't anticipated a situation like that at all, despite David's near promises that something would go horribly wrong and her life would be endangered. Yet it was really just a culmination of everything that had happened in Selma. And despite the accompanying fear and worry, there was still something exhilarating about her experiences, a validation of sorts for her own work. Not that she needed it, or was looking for trouble, but she realized that every dark moment she encountered made the movement real in a way that it hadn't been before. She knew the risk that she was taking when she first boarded the plane in New York, and there were times that she did wonder whether she would make it back alive. But she also didn't want to travel all the way to Selma without seeing what the movement was really like, even in its ugliest, most vile form.

"I'm hanging in there," she said to Leroy. "There was another girl from New York last night, a volunteer who was kinda off her rocker a bit, but other than that it wasn't so bad." Bev caught a whiff of some bacon Leroy had just started in another pan. "I am definitely starving, though."

"Well, I sure am glad to hear that." Leroy laughed. "I been wonderin' how you been gettin' by on coffee and cigarettes anyhow. Hold tight, 'cause I'll have some bacon and eggs and home fries ready in a minute."

"I can't wait."

"So the girl from New York," Leroy asked. "What was her deal?"

"To be honest, I'm not really sure," Bev said. "She first had a problem when the leaders separated the men and women and made us sleep on different floors. Then she kept going on about how the leadership is comprised mostly of men, and she feels they don't have the same level of respect for the women in the movement."

"I see. And what do you think about that?" Leroy paused from pouring cornmeal into a small bowl where he was mixing up a quick hoecake batter. He seemed genuinely interested in her response, but Bev wanted him to keep cooking. If breakfast was like this in New York, she might be willing to actually eat it more often.

"The men in leadership definitely have very strong personalities, but I honestly haven't been here long enough to know whether her claims are valid," Bev said. "I will say, though, that I met Amelia Boynton at the second march, and she seemed to be truly revered by all of the leaders."

"So you sayin' she was overreacting?"

"I won't go that far," Bev answered. "I don't think it's ever right to diminish someone's feelings, and if she has truly been treated unfairly simply because she's a woman, that should be addressed. But I hesitate to take the focus away from what matters here and from what we're doing tomorrow.

"Ultimately, I believe that her actions last night may have done that. So instead of spending all of our time strategizing our next steps and brainstorming ways to continue to force the establishment to take notice of the injustices that are occurring here, we—or I, more specifically—had to convince this woman to take the focus off herself and to redirect it toward the people we're here to help. I just don't feel that that's a conversation I should have had to have. And that's what makes Mrs. Boynton such a special woman. Her picture was on the front page of every newspaper in America, but she never made the issue about her—it's about the movement."

"So what happened after y'all talked?"

"Christine? Oh, she decided she wanted to be alone, so she moved her cot over to a corner where she could be away from everyone else, and it was probably for the best. She was disrespectful and unruly, and things would have gotten completely out of control if other people noticed her behavior and thought they could act that way, too."

"Well at least you were there, Miss Beverly," Leroy said as he laid the plate of smoking-hot food on the table in front of her. "Sounds like you had everything under control. And it seems like you've been learnin' a lot down here with us country folk." Leroy grinned at her, his perfect, white teeth shining against his dark skin.

"Actually, I have," Bev said with a mouthful of potatoes. "I knew that I wanted to be a part of this, but I don't think I knew why, initially. It felt like the right thing to do, even though I couldn't justify to my friends back home why I would be willing to risk my life when they weren't willing to make that commitment.

"But I know now that I *needed* to be here," she continued. "Being a part of the movement has changed my life. The way I see and understand the human experience is completely different, and that will forever impact my work going forward."

⌐◦⌐

The afternoon of Sunday, March 21, was unseasonably cool for Alabama, with temperatures hovering in the forties. But that didn't stop the more than five thousand people who were gathered at Brown Chapel, many wearing long wool coats, hats, and gloves. Most of them were black—and there was a strong contingent of local, Selma citizens—but there were also whites, as well as Latinos and Asians. And just beyond the large crowd was a group of hundreds of federalized Alabama National Guardsmen and FBI agents. Even more were in cars that were lined up on the street, ready to go out both in front of and behind the marchers.

It was clear that, despite the violence of the first march that took place a full two weeks prior on March 7, and the disappointment of being turned around on March 9, the people of Selma and their supporters from around the country knew that things would be different that day. There was a sense of confidence and jubilation in the air, well before anyone took one step toward Montgomery. Women were laughing and singing while men slapped backs.

Bev stood off to the side of the church, taking it all in. After she'd finished Leroy's breakfast the previous day, she spent more than five hours at the church meticulously screening the marchers to select those who would be a part of the three hundred allowed to march on days two and three, on the two-lane stretch of Highway 80 between Selma and Montgomery.

The march was carefully organized to include local leadership, as well as representatives from various civil rights groups around the country. But leaders were clear that of the three hundred, 278 were to be local Selma and Alabama citizens, with preference given to all those who had been in the first march. With the number of participants swelling, many people were upset about being turned away, but Bev knew, unmistakably, that this was the right decision. This was *their* march and *their* petition to the governor.

So Bev and the other social workers were tasked with making sure those who were chosen most embodied the ideals of the movement, ideals that Bev had only recently begun to understand fully herself.

While MCHR workers evaluated the physical health of marchers, checking for any serious conditions such as high blood pressure or joint pain that might prevent them from being on their feet for an extended period of time, Bev assessed their mental health. Using the list of questions from George, the social workers were to look for any signs of aggression or unwillingness to follow orders. Those would cause an immediate dismissal, as would a history of violence. "Dr. King doesn't want any crazy people marching," Walter had told them.

Anna Hockett was an olive-skinned housewife from Michigan with three kids who was so desperate to march that she drove all the way to Selma by herself. "Some of my closest friends don't know this," she told Bev, "but my paternal grandfather was a black man who grew up not too far from here. I feel such a connection to these people that I had to help."

It broke Bev's heart to tell Anna that she would only be able to march part of the distance, because of the three hundred spots to go all the way to Montgomery, the twenty-two that were reserved for out-of-towners were already filled.

"I'm sorry, but there's really nothing I can do," Bev said.

Anna's eyes welled with tears. "Miss, I understand that this may be out of your hands, as far as me being allowed to march. But please don't tell me I've come all this way for nothing. I just can't imagine walking a few miles today and then going home."

Bev talked to Walter, who then spoke with Father Neil, and ultimately, they were able to find something else for her to do. She was going to drive ahead to Montgomery and help shuttle marchers back to Selma in her car.

But aside from the occasional case like Anna's, in which nonlocals had to be turned away, Bev didn't come across any difficulties in her screenings. There was no one whose disposition was in blatant opposition to the movement, because by that point, it seemed, all the potential marchers were aware of the beliefs of Dr. King and the other movement leaders, and they could also recognize their effectiveness. The murmurs of doubt and concern over Dr. King's decision to turn back during the second march had been replaced by words of confirmation and support, especially after the president's public declaration backing their efforts.

Case in point: Bev met a woman named Tandy whose thirteen-year-old son had been beaten by one of Jim Clark's deputies that first Sunday. She'd picked up her son's bloodied body from the asphalt and carried him in her arms until a stranger introduced himself, took the boy, and carried him in his arms. He drove Tandy and her son back to their home, where she spent two days nursing his wounds. With a testimony like that, Bev expected to find a woman who was angry and bitter, ready to rail against the authorities and the nonviolent credo that rendered her son defenseless. But Tandy was none of those things. "The good Lord always gon' protect his children," she told Bev. "These cuts and bruises ain't nothin' like the pain he gon' feel if we don't stand up and make a change now."

People with stories like Tandy's were a constant that day, as screening after screening turned up individuals who had been harassed and beaten, but who were determined to fight back with their feet instead of their hands. Now Bev watched the crowd of anxious marchers as they waited on the church grounds for the signal to begin. There was a small group of men standing at the top of the stairs near the entrance to Brown Chapel, and as one of them began speaking Bev recognized him as Jimmie Lee's grandfather.

"I can't believe how many of y'all are here today," Mr. Lee started, clearly emotional. "I know if my grandson was here today, he would be so proud to see y'all standin' up and fightin' for what's yours." He paused to wipe his eyes before continuing. "Some of y'all may not know this, but I'm a little up in age." The old man smiled while the crowd laughed. "But Jimmie Lee, that boy was smart. He told me it ain't ever too late for me to make a difference. Well, he was right. That's why I'm here today."

Mr. Lee's eyes scanned the mass of people standing below

him. "I'm telling you, it ain't ever too late for you, either. After this is over, when you leave and go back to wherever home is, remember this moment. Remember the power that you have—the power that we have as a group—and use it. No matter what you're up against, you can make a difference."

Days before the march began, members of the SCLC had reached out to Negro landowners with properties along the predetermined route who would be willing to let marchers camp on their land overnight. The first day, after marchers traveled around eight miles, they stayed at the farm of David Hall. Then, the next morning, as protestors neared the Dallas/Lowndes county line where Highway 80 narrowed, the vast majority of the marchers had to leave by car. Many returned to Selma, while others, including Bev, drove to Montgomery, where they would wait for the others.

The remaining marchers spent the second night on the property of Rosie Steele and the third at the Robert Gardner Farm. On the fourth night, the City of St. Jude, a Catholic Church complex, welcomed the demonstrators, becoming the only organization, or nonindividual, to do so. Later, the church would lose many of its supporters because of its goodwill toward the movement, but on the night of March 24, there was only joy in the air. The popular singer and actor Harry Belafonte organized the Stars for Freedom concert, which featured Sammy Davis Jr., Tony Bennett, Nina Simone, and others.

On the fifth and final day of the march, there were nearly twenty-five thousand marchers making the final trek to the Alabama state capitol building, including the celebrities who had entertained them the night before. Along the way, Bev held hands with a woman from Vermont and a man from Kansas. They sang and cried and basked in the momentous occasion.

Once they arrived at the capitol, Dr. King addressed the enormous crowd, quickly and eloquently capturing the travails of the march.

"We have walked through desolate valleys and across the trying hills. We have walked on meandering highways and rested our bodies on rocky byways."

As always when Dr. King spoke, the people were nodding and raising hands as his words moved them.

"But today as I stand before you and think back over that great march, I can say, as Sister Pollard, a seventy-year-old Negro woman who lived in this community during the bus boycott, once said, our feet are tired, but our souls are rested," Dr. King said.

Shouts of "Well!" and "Yes, sir!" rang out from the audience.

Bev looked around at the mass of people and at Dr. King, the most influential leader of the civil rights movement. He, along with the army of construction workers around her, was rebuilding the South. And she was a part of it. The country was on the cusp of real change, and she was partially responsible for making it happen.

"Once more the method of nonviolent resistance was unsheathed from its scabbard, and once again an entire community was mobilized to confront the adversary," Dr. King said forcefully.

Bev listened with a special pleasure as Dr. King went on to speak of the president.

"A president born in the South had the sensitivity to feel the will of the country, and in an address that will live in history as one of the most passionate pleas for human rights ever made by a president of our nation, he pledged the might of the federal government to cast off the centuries-old blight. President Johnson rightly praised the courage of the Negro for awakening the conscience of the nation."

Bev remembered the look of pure joy on Leroy's face as he hurried off to open the Sweet Spot so the Negroes of Selma could celebrate the fact that the president, who had once ignored their plight, was now completely behind them. He and Essie Mae were somewhere in the crowd, she knew, no doubt grinning from ear to ear.

The crowd was roaring as Dr. King settled into his trademark cadence.

"Yes, we are on the move, and no wave of racism can stop us. We are on the move now. The burning of our churches will not deter us. The bombing of our homes will not dissuade us. We are on the move now. The beating and killing of our clergymen and young people will not divert us. We are on the move now. The wanton release of their known murderers would not discourage us. We are on the move now. Like an idea whose time has come, not even the marching of mighty armies can halt us. We are moving to the land of freedom."

THIRTEEN

THREE WEEKS AFTER Bev first boarded a plane to Alabama, she was in an almost identical position, sandwiched between the window of the jet on her right and Mary on her left. The pilot announced that they were ready for takeoff, and Bev felt the wheels lift from the ground and fold under the plane's belly while she watched as Alabama's capital city grew smaller and smaller beneath her window until, finally, only clouds could be seen.

Just as the Birmingham landscape had disappeared before her eyes, Bev understood that she was also saying good-bye to a moment in time that would impact not only her life, but also the future of the country for many years to come. Her role was only minor in relation to the magnitude of the much bigger production—the production that had been orchestrated well before she arrived and that would continue well after she departed—but she was grateful, nonetheless. She was grateful that she had been blessed with the opportunity to be a part of the movement, and perhaps more important, she felt blessed to have had the foresight to take advantage of the opportunity as soon as it presented itself. It would have been easy to consider it someone else's battle to fight, to stay in the comfort and safety of the little corner of the universe she had claimed for herself. But she would have missed the fantastic chance to save lives and change lives—hers chief among them.

Bev smelled the aroma wafting from the paper bags she and Mary had wedged under their seats. She grabbed hers, opening the top to take in the full scent of the fried chicken. Since she and Mary kept raving about it after Leroy cooked it for their dinner in Selma, he insisted on making more for their trip home. Mary reached for her lunch, too, and for a while they sat quietly, only the sounds of their smacking and the hum of the plane's engine filling the space between them.

"Well, it's over. Back to New York," Bev said between chews as Mary nodded in agreement. "Any idea what's next?"

Mary sucked the last piece of meat from the leg bone before dropping it back in the bag. Then she pulled out a slice of sweet potato pie covered in plastic wrap. "I'm not sure," she said. "I've actually been thinking about coming back to Alabama if I can't find a job after graduation. I talked to Walter, and he said there's still a lot of work to be done. Now that the voting rights bill has been introduced, I guess they're going to focus on the health care system and try to create more facilities and care providers in Selma."

"Right. Because if Minister Reeb had been able to see a doctor in Selma, he might still be alive."

"Exactly," Mary said.

"That's great; I'm really happy for you!" Bev gave Mary a slight nudge with her shoulder. "But, remember, I still want you to call me. And not just about your internship. If it doesn't work out for you to come back to Alabama after graduation, or if you decide that you'd rather stay in New York, give me a call. If I can't work out anything with my connections, I'm sure we can find something for you at SWCRA."

"Thanks, Bev," Mary said with an appreciative smile.

It was hard to believe that less than a month before, the two women barely knew each other. Now, after weeks of sharing a bed and lots of secrets, they were as close as lifelong best friends.

"What about you?" Mary asked. "Are you planning to stay in the movement?"

"I'm not really sure," Bev said, looking at the clouds that looked like giant-size cotton balls. "I'm definitely still going to be working with SWCRA, but I don't know what else I'll be doing." She shifted her hips just slightly, enough so that she could turn to face Mary. "Going to Selma really changed my perspective on a lot of things. The problems we saw there weren't just about race, though I'm sure everything else stems from that root. But there are social justice issues just as compelling. I think it's amazing what you guys are going to do to provide quality health care for people who may have never even been to the doctor or dentist in their entire lives, and that kind of work—helping people gain access to the basic necessities of life—is the work that I want to continue doing."

Bev thought back to Sarah Toombs and all the other people she met who were struggling from day to day just to survive. The media had done a great job capturing the wild antics of Jim Clark and other staunch segregationists who were so set in their dispositions that they didn't care about being photographed while beating an elderly woman over the head with a nightstick. But Bev had learned that racism didn't always show up with bells on, announcing its presence before it ever entered the room. Bev knew now that there was a much more pervasive— and perhaps more dangerous—form.

Senators could write laws that require officials to allow Negroes to vote or ride buses in whatever seat they choose. But it wasn't nearly as easy to address the perceptions and prejudices that so many whites held—prejudices that would prevent Negroes from being hired by whites for jobs they qualified for, or that would keep them from being able to buy a house they could afford in a neighborhood occupied by whites. Secretly, Bev wondered whether those problems would ever be solved, or whether her feelings that the mountain was just too insurmountable would prove to be true.

In fifty years, as Americans celebrated the great march from Selma to Montgomery and President Johnson's speech on voters' rights, would the country still be ensnared in the traps of racism's stealthiest forms?

"So what do you think happened to George?" Mary said, breaking Bev out of her thoughts.

For the most part, Bev had gotten really good at not thinking much about George at all, as she purposely reminded herself that he was a soldier with a greater purpose—a worker in Dr. King's construction company rebuilding the South—and that no news was good news. "I try not to dwell on it too much," she explained.

"I'm so sorry, Bev," Mary said, placing her hand on top of her friend's. "You guys were really starting to hit it off, and it's just so sad that something terrible could have happened, and we have no idea at all about it."

Bev nodded solemnly.

"Did you hear about the housewife from Michigan?" Mary asked, continuing.

"Are you talking about Anna Hockett?"

"I think that's her name. She was darker skinned with really long, brown hair and a mole above her left eyebrow . . ."

"Yes," Bev said. "I screened her. What happened?"

"Well, you know she was shuttling marchers back to Selma . . . I guess the KKK followed her, and they shot and killed her."

"Oh my gosh!" Bev said, aghast, clapping her hand over her mouth. "I had no idea. That's terrible!"

Bev shook her head and remembered when Dr. K. asked whether she'd be willing to give up her involvement in the movement for her future husband. And she thought about David's attempts to convince her not to go to Selma. She wondered whether Anna's husband supported her decision to leave.

"Are you dating anyone?" Bev asked Mary.

"Nooo . . . why?" Mary looked at Bev curiously, as if she had pieces of fried chicken skin stuck to her cheeks. "Is this about George? Because I've already thought about that, and I don't think I would ever date anyone working in the movement. I can't imagine how stressful it would be to always be worried and wondering when he would come home—*if* he would come home."

"Right," Bev said, looking directly into Mary's eyes. "But it's not just about *you* making a decision not to date someone working in the South. You have to also understand that a man you're interested in may not be interested in you if you're still active."

Bev watched as Mary's eyes fell and she clasped her hands together on her lap. Bev's point was obviously something she hadn't considered before. "Think about how passionate you feel right now, how much you're dying to get back to help even more people, and ask yourself if you could give it all up—if you *would* give it all up—just because someone asked you to."

Mary waited a couple of beats, as if carefully formulating her response. Then she said, matter-of-factly, "I believe that I made this trip for a reason. Rebelling against my parents has become secondary to making an impact. I honestly believe that if it is time for me to get married, if I meet the man I'm supposed to spend the rest of my life with, he will understand that and be more than supportive. I just can't see it any other way."

Bev barely had her key out of the lock before her roommates rushed to the door to greet her.

"Oh my gosh, Bev!" Barbara squealed as she wrapped Bev in a tight embrace. "You've been gone sooo long! We saw on TV that there was a third march." And, then, with a more serious tone, she asked, "Why haven't you called?"

The wheels of Bev's mind started turning as she tried to think of a response that would pacify her friends. She knew that she didn't want them to worry or question why she'd decided to stay in Selma for a few weeks instead of a few days. If they had been concerned about her safety before, it certainly wouldn't have helped to tell them there had been an injunction forbidding them from marching on the ninth, that they wouldn't be able to try again until they received federal support, and that, in the meantime, she'd be living in the heart of the Negro community among the very people who were regularly intimidated and terrorized by local whites.

But despite Bev's decision to cut off communication from Selma, she'd forgotten about the power of the press.

"It's a long story," Bev said to Barbara. She hung her wool coat on the rack next to the door and then flopped onto the couch, cigarette in hand.

"Well, tell us what it was like," Barbara said, sitting next to her.

"It was incredible," Bev replied, lighting her cigarette. "There's really no way to describe it. It was a once-in-a-lifetime opportunity, really. The people, the marching, the whole experience was just incredible."

"Okay, so it was incredible. But you have to tell us more than that! Details, details," Barbara said anxiously.

"Well, I stayed with this wonderful couple while I was in town. They owned a restaurant, and the husband—his name is Leroy—did all the cooking. Best fried chicken *ever*. By the way, did you know that restaurants in the South serve iced tea that is already sweet?"

"I think I heard something about that," Marianne said from the armchair in the corner of the room. "Keep going."

"So, Leroy, he spoke with this completely broken English, but it was so endearing. And he was so intelligent—and I don't mean 'intelligent for a Negro,' but *really* brilliant. And Dr. King.

Everything you've heard or read or seen about him is completely true. Each time he spoke, it was so well planned. He completely captivated every audience. And he was the same one-on-one. I met him right after the second march and he just had this aura of greatness. The man quotes Shakespeare, for goodness' sake. I'm sure generations from now, kids will be studying his speeches in college English classes."

"Wow. I wish I could have been there." Barbara's face was plastered with a huge grin.

Bev paused before responding. "Actually, you could have been there—or don't you remember?" she said, effectively wiping away Barbara's smile.

"I see you haven't changed a bit," Marianne snapped.

Bev ignored her. "So what's been going on around here?"

"You haven't noticed anything different?" Barbara said, resting her left hand on Bev's lap in a very obvious way. She didn't seem too bothered by Bev's thinly veiled insult.

"Barbara!" Bev shouted. "Congratulations!" Bev picked up Barbara's hand to get a better look at the diamond solitaire gleaming on her ring finger. "Tell me everything!"

"Well . . ." Barbara said, blushing. "I told you John's parents were driving down to have dinner with us? Well, he proposed that night! I had no idea, but I guess he had already spoken to Marianne to get my ring size."

Marianne nodded her head to confirm.

"That's great, really," Bev said, hugging her friend. "I am so happy for you." She broke her embrace, then asked, "What are his parents like?"

"I like them a lot. They're a little old-fashioned, though. His mom, Mrs. Friedman, doesn't work. Apparently, she has a PhD in English lit and she was teaching at NYU, but once she got married, and then got pregnant with John's older sister, she stopped working. Her dad didn't think it was appropriate for her to continue working outside of the home when she had a family to care for and he was doing well enough financially to support them."

"They told you that?" Bev asked incredulously.

"Of course not! That's just what John told me after dinner, to fill in the gaps and, I guess, to let me know what his expectations are for me."

"So he doesn't want you to work?" Bev laughed as she tried to imagine her friend spending her days vacuuming and baking cookies.

"We haven't really talked about it in detail, but probably not." Barbara was twisting her engagement ring in a continuous loop around her finger.

"Are you okay with that?" Bev asked. "I mean, you do have a career, after all. And what about your patients? Are they supposed to be okay with you leaving them just because you're getting married?"

"Goodness, Bev! What's gotten into you?" Marianne said,

butting in. "Out of all of us, you were the one most ready to get married, and I'm pretty sure you considered that your husband may want you to stop working. So why are you being so mean to Barbara?"

"It's fine," Barbara said. "Bev is probably just tired from her trip."

"No, I'm not tired," Bev snapped. "I just think that sometimes a woman's work is too fulfilling and meaningful to leave it behind for a man." She thought back to her conversation with Mary on the plane. "I still want to be married, but is it so wrong for me to want my husband to be supportive of my life and what I do?"

"Okay, enough of that," Barbara said, still trying to ease the tension. "Speaking of men, guess who's been by here no less than a dozen times looking for you?"

"Who?" Bev asked, genuinely curious.

"David, of course!" Barbara said playfully. "Who were you expecting me to say?"

George, Bev thought. At least that was who she'd hoped had been by. Maybe he wasn't missing at all, and he just decided to head back north without telling anyone. Then, when he thought Bev had made it back home, he wanted to surprise her. But just as quickly as the thought came, she forced it out of her mind and back into the realm of make-believe, where it belonged.

"He didn't call first?" Bev asked.

"No, he did. Probably twenty times. I guess he thought we

were lying when we said you weren't back in town yet, so he wanted to come over and see for himself. What's going on? Didn't you talk to him while you were in Selma?"

Bev had purposely decided not to call David, either. She was trying to avoid dealing with the fallout from the open discussion of their very nonexistent romance for as long as possible.

"I didn't," Bev said. "There was no way I could have known before I left that the second march wouldn't be completed, and that we'd have to wait more than ten days before we could finish it. Plus, while we waited, we were busy anyway, going into the community trying to register voters. I just really didn't have time to talk to him."

Marianne and Barbara wore matching looks of complete and utter disbelief.

"Why are you looking at me like that?" Bev asked, attempting to evade their knowing stares.

"Beverly Luther," Marianne started. "Do you have any idea how well I know you? I can tell when you're hiding something."

"Marianne Furr," Bev retorted. "Do you have any idea how much you sound like my mother?"

"Well, if I sound like your mother, have some respect and tell us what's really going on."

Bev looked back and forth between them while she contemplated how much she should share. "Look, it's nothing. Really. David and I just had a little disagreement before I left."

"About what?" Barbara was shocked. "I've never seen you guys argue, and I haven't noticed any kind of conflict within SWCRA."

"It wasn't about work," Bev said flatly.

"What then?"

"Something more personal . . ."

"You know, I knew this would happen," Marianne said arrogantly. "Everyone can see how he looks at you. So let me guess—he said that he wanted to take your relationship to the next level, and you shot him down." She was laughing now. "Who knew you could be so heartless, Bev. I mean, you should've seen how pitiful he looked."

Marianne thought she had it all figured out, but Barbara knew better. She saw Bev's solemn face, the way she sat, unmoved, while Marianne was doubled over in laughter, and she pressed for more. "Are you sure everything is okay?" Barbara asked.

"It's fine," Bev said. "Marianne's just got it wrong, that's all. David *did* say that he had feelings for me, but he also said that we couldn't be in a relationship—at least not one that would end in marriage."

"Well, why on earth not?" Marianne said, momentarily pausing her giggles. "You guys would make such a cute couple." Then, not able to resist: "Is it because you talk so much he could never get a word in? No, wait—it's because he doesn't want you to be his boss at work and at home, right?"

Marianne's laughter started up again, but Bev wasn't offended by her friend's amusement. It really was some sick joke, she thought. She and David did make a cute couple, and they would be great together.

"Wrong again," Bev said sarcastically. "He doesn't want to date me because I'm white."

Marianne's chin dropped. "Can you repeat that?"

"Which part?"

"I'm serious, Bev." Marianne left her seat in the corner of the room and wedged herself onto the couch between Bev and Barbara. "I just can't believe that. Did he try to explain himself?"

"Not really," Bev said. "I mean, I was hurt at first, of course. Maybe I still am, at least a little bit anyway." She reached for another cigarette from the pack sitting on the end table. "Obviously, I was very upset when it first happened. But now . . . I don't know . . ."

"You don't know what?" Marianne was glaring at Bev with wide eyes, waiting for her to say something that could justify what seemed like a completely hypocritical sentiment coming from a man who spent his career fighting for civil rights.

"I just get it now," Bev said. "I spent three weeks in the Deep South, and I saw how he grew up. The men there, the Negroes, they are considered less than human. And interracial mixing, that's the ultimate sin."

"Okay, sure. But this isn't the South, Bev."

"I said the same thing, before I knew. And it's not that his position is right or wrong. It just *is*. We are all products of our respective environments and creatures of the influences that shaped us. We all have different perspectives, and I can only respect his."

Bev arrived at the SWCRA offices earlier than usual the next morning—partly because she was anxious to see whether she'd received any important messages while she was away, and partly because she knew David would already be there.

David was an early riser, typically finishing his coffee and the morning paper by six thirty, and sure enough, at seven o'clock he was already in the office, dressed in dark gray slacks and a pale blue cable-knit sweater. Bev took a moment to look at him through the window in the office door, to watch him as his long frame eased across the small room, first filing away a stack of papers, then sliding another stack into a large, padded envelope to be mailed. He was every bit as handsome as she remembered, his thick brows knitted in concentration as he worked, while his sweater gripped the muscles in his arms and shoulders just slightly.

Finally, Bev turned the knob on the door and stepped inside.

"Bev!" David ran to her with a look of both relief and concern on his face. He wrapped his arms around her and held her close enough for Bev to inhale the scent of his aftershave. "I've called and been to your house so many times. When I heard that the march had been rescheduled for the twenty-first, I wasn't sure if you were staying, but when you never came back I assumed that you did. But why didn't you call? I've been so worried!"

Just then Bev realized that maybe her plan of avoidance wasn't the right one. She hadn't considered that he could have been genuinely concerned about her safety; she could relate to that nerve-wracking feeling firsthand, and she didn't wish for anyone else to experience that.

"I'm sorry . . . I was just so busy . . ."

"Okay . . ." David dropped his arms and stepped back to look Bev in the eyes. "Well, tell me all about it. I want to know exactly what it was like."

Bev and David sat in two chairs near the door, and Bev proceeded to tell him all about Leroy and Essie Mae, and Jimmie Lee's grandfather and Brown Chapel. She told him about the sweet tea at the Sweet Spot, and she told him about the night at the community center and about marching among thousands of people, all united by one singular goal. Finally, she told him about going door-to-door in Perry and Dallas Counties and the incredible challenges so many of the people were facing there.

"Working with Walter and the Medical Committee for

Human Rights was a marvelous experience," Bev said. "Interestingly enough, the doctors didn't involve themselves with anything in terms of social action, but the social workers did, and I was glad. I am proud of the work I did, and hopefully social work may really stand for social action—in the real sense of the word—someday."

"Sure," David replied. "And in terms of the civil rights movement, we have so much more to give and to understand. With what's going on in the world, all the injustices against people, the social work profession has been out of it. We need to step up and give more, but I don't know if we're ready to."

Bev nodded silently, thinking about the first few days she listened to the problems of the people she met, how they couldn't feed their kids or couldn't get a fair trial for a loved one or had been repeatedly denied government assistance. In every case, initially, she thanked them for their time and turned right back around and walked out the door, leaving them still drowning in hopelessness. But finally getting up and helping Sarah Toombs find a solution to her problems had empowered Bev in a way she hadn't expected.

"One of the pastors there gave quite a damning speech on social work," Bev said. "SCLC will be coming into Harlem next summer and he said, 'Within three months we will do more for Harlem than all the social workers there have done for the last twenty years.' And of course he's right. He's absolutely right. In terms of group community action and community organization, we are so far behind it's pathetic."

The two sat in silence for a moment, taking in the gravity of Bev's statements.

"Well, Bev," David said as he reached out to touch Bev's hand, "I just want to tell you that I'm glad you were able to go to Selma. I gained a lot of respect for you—not in terms of me respecting you as a person, because I already had that, but because you had an experience that I wish I could have had."

Bev looked back at David in amazement. Where was this coming from? Hadn't she tried to convince him to go? And hadn't he, in turn, tried to make her stay?

"You know my buddy Donald, from undergrad? Well, I saw him and his little girl about a week after you left, and she asked me why I didn't go to Selma. She's only ten or eleven, but she knows that I'm active in the movement, and she's old enough to understand that something special was going on down there, so she wanted to know why I wasn't a part of it."

"What did you say?" Bev asked.

"I told the truth. I said I just didn't have the guts to go."

Bev was stunned by his admission. "Wow, David. I don't know what to say."

"I thought about it a lot while you were gone," David said, now pacing around the room. "The things that happened in my childhood, and to Mickey, they've stayed with me. I can't help that, and I just didn't have the courage to go, and I think I kind of resented you for having the courage to do what I couldn't." He stopped walking and kneeled in front of Bev. "You've always been so confident and sure of yourself. That's one of the things I love most about you—"

"Listen, David," Bev said as she jumped up from her seat, suddenly uncomfortable. "I totally understand where you were coming from. Different people are called to different areas of the movement, and that's okay."

"I know, but it's not just that." David's breathing was shallow and labored, as if he'd just jogged a couple of miles. "The conversation we had right before you left . . . I wanted to talk about it . . . I know I may have hurt you . . ."

Bev's head was swimming. She wasn't sure why she felt so uneasy about the topic of conversation, or why the truth of David's unwillingness to go to Selma had somehow changed her perception of him and their relationship.

"It's fine, really," she said, walking across the room to open a window, despite the fact that the outside temperature was barely above freezing. She pulled at the top of her turtleneck to try to let some air in. Then she turned around and David was behind her, still nervous and fidgety.

"You're not mad, are you?" he asked. "I just want to make sure things are fine between us. The last thing I ever wanted to do was hurt you; you mean so much—"

David was cut off again, but this time by the phone on Bev's desk. She raced to answer it, thankful for the interruption.

"This is Beverly speaking," she said into the receiver. She paused a moment before adding, "Oh, hi, Walter. How are you?"

From across the room, David could see Bev's expression change from pleasant to anguished, though he couldn't hear what Walter was saying on the other end. And truthfully, Bev couldn't make out much of it either. All the words seemed to run together, tripping on top of one another: *George found, body burned, no suspects.*

Bev hung up the phone and tried to piece the fragments together in her mind. Could Walter's words really be true? If the body was burned, how could they be sure it was George?

"What's wrong?" David asked, as Bev stood still, frozen in place.

Bev turned to look at him through eyes blurred by a wall of water. "Nothing. Everything is fine," she lied.

David didn't believe her. "Okay . . ." he said. "And what about us . . . You sure you're not mad?"

Bev thought about her answer. "Of course not, David. How could I be mad?" she said, offering a shaky smile. "Life is just *too short* to be upset." Then she blinked, and the tears came crashing down her cheeks.

FOURTEEN

Bᴇᴠ ᴛᴏᴏᴋ ᴏɴᴇ last glance at her notes on the lectern and then squinted under the harsh auditorium lights as she looked out at the sea of faces staring back at her. While others in her position may have been nervous about speaking in front of such a large and distinguished audience, Bev was relaxed and at ease. She took a deep breath and smoothed the front of her suit jacket.

"Good evening, ladies and gentlemen," Bev said. "It is my honor and pleasure to introduce the keynote speaker of the 1966 Medical Committee for Human Rights National Convention."

Bev paused and smiled for a bit, to ramp up the crowd's anticipation. "About a year ago, I traveled from my home in New York to Selma, Alabama, to participate in the Selma-to-Montgomery voters' rights marches. Like many of you who have worked in the South, I experienced a bit of culture shock. And I was overwhelmed by the magnitude of the problems facing Negroes in Alabama. But one of the key factors in my commitment to effect real change while I was in Selma in March of 1965—as well as my dedication to continue that work even after I left— was the man who is about to come to the stage.

"I had heard lots about him before I ever arrived in Selma," Bev continued. "As one of the most prominent leaders in the civil rights movement, this man commands full attention wherever he goes. So imagine my surprise when he told me that he had heard about me—a regular white girl from Brooklyn by way of San Francisco. But he did, and when I met him that first time, he let me know how valuable I was to the movement and how impressed he was that I had traveled to Selma."

Bev stopped for a moment and let the memory of that day in front of Brown Chapel sink in. She was speaking from a place of authenticity, and she wanted her true emotion to shine through her words.

"That sense of empowerment that Dr. King gave me is the same one he conveys every time he stands on a stage or on a pulpit," Bev said. "It is the notion that each and every person, no matter how average or insignificant, can make a difference. And, in fact, it is often the most simple among us who have the greatest impact—like the weary seamstress who was just too tired to give up her seat on a Montgomery bus.

"And I know that after you hear him speak this evening, you will walk away with a passion and determination far exceeding what you came in with, and it is with that that you will be the catalysts for the next great wave of change in this country."

Bev paused one final time and let a wide smile cover her face. "So without further ado, I'd like to introduce . . . Dr. Martin Luther King Junior!"

Bev gathered her stack of notes, and as she walked over to the side of the stage, she waited for Dr. King to approach. "It's so nice to see you again," she said, hugging him.

"And it's a pleasure to see you as well," Dr. King said, hugging her back. "Thank you so much for the gracious introduction."

Outside the auditorium, Bev was looking for the restroom when she spotted Walter.

"How have you been?" she asked, as her small frame was wrapped in another embrace.

"I'm great. And thank you so much for agreeing to come and speak on such short notice. Dr. King requested you, specifically."

"I had no idea," Bev said, blushing. "Well, thank you for inviting me. There's no way I would have missed this." Her tone grew serious as she said, "I'm sorry I couldn't make it to the service last month. I just don't think I'm ready."

Walter's eyes softened with sympathy. "I understand, Bev. I think George's death was hard on everyone. You know the risks, sure, but you still don't really expect anything to happen to you or anyone you know." He sighed. "The memorial was beautiful, though."

There was an uncomfortable silence as memories of George washed over Bev. They shared so few moments over the short time she knew him so the memories that remained were especially strong and vivid—even a full year later.

"So I heard you're working with Mobilization for Youth in Manhattan now," Walter said, trying to ease the tension.

"Yes. Yes, I am," Bev replied. "I was with Hillside Hospital for five years, and after I returned from Selma, I was really longing for a job that was more community focused."

"And you feel like you have that in your new position?"

"Absolutely."

Under President Johnson, the Office of Economic Opportunity and the City of New York had recently launched Mobilization for Youth (MFY) as a pioneering project on New York's Lower East Side. The aim was to have a more significant—and early—impact on the lives of at-risk children. The program, which was the first of its kind, was "a multidisciplinary social agency geared to demonstration, research, and social action in eradicating poverty and its attendant ills" and was called "a watershed in the development of social welfare in America."

Bev's responsibilities included the research and writing of articles documenting the organization's services. They were compiled in the document "Individual and Group Services in the Mobilization for Youth Experience" and were later published in Volume I of the *New Social Work* series. Her articles documented the successes and failures of their services, and while Bev found the writing difficult and dreaded the task, she knew it had to be done.

By far, Bev's favorite part of the job was recruiting and supervising social agencies and personnel to carry out the educational and social action missions of MFY. Under the broad rubric of "providing opportunities," MFY contracted with churches, synagogues, and settlement houses to provide social outreach to children and adolescents who were in gangs or considered at risk for delinquency. The programs themselves were wide-ranging and included the Pre-Adolescent Program, which discouraged younger children from imitating the behavior of teenage gang members by offering attractive alternatives; the Detached Worker Program, which hired social workers to go out on the streets to meet gangs, in effect creating a bridge between gang members and school authorities, courts, employers, and police; and several education programs, which were designed to bring preschool to second-grade children up to grade level.

"That's great," Walter said. "I'm glad to hear that you've found something that keeps you excited about going to work every day, and that also impacts the lives of so many others."

"Well, honestly, you're partly responsible for that," Bev said. "If you had never asked me to go to Selma, and I had never seen the real work that needed to be done in the communities, I probably never would have considered taking a job like this. So, now, thanks to you, I'm able to help not just Negroes, but all poor and vulnerable people in New York."

Walter smiled. "I really don't know how much credit I can take, Bev. I think it's just a testament to your spirit and good-will." He stopped and pulled a sheet of paper from the portfolio he was holding. "I wanted to give you this," he said, handing the paper to Bev.

"What is this?"

"It's an official letter from MCHR, inviting you to become our national secretary. The board has already voted, and the decision was unanimous. All we need now is your acceptance."

"Oh my goodness, Walter!" Bev was stunned as she held the page in her hands and skimmed over the text. She looked back up at Walter. "I'm not even a physician. Isn't that a requirement for becoming a national officer?"

"Not anymore," Walter replied. "We have been so impressed by your work and we've all come to understand the importance of social work in the larger civil rights movement. It would be a shame to prohibit someone of your skill level from taking a more active role in the organization because of some outdated practice."

"Wow . . . thanks . . ." Bev was flattered and still in shock. "I don't know what to say."

"Well, say yes, then."

"Okay, Walter," Bev said, laughing. "Yes. I'd love to be the new national secretary for the Medical Committee for Human Rights."

As if she hadn't already been busy enough, Bev's schedule only intensified after taking the position with MCHR, and she was speaking more than ever. In May she was a main speaker at the Social Work Student Forum in New York, where she spoke to students from five graduate schools on the topic "Social Work and the Poverty Program." Later, at the end of the month, she was the sole representative from MFY to attend the National Conference on Social Welfare, where she also spoke.

In addition to making a name for herself, Bev was also making a considerable amount of money in consultation and speaking fees. The YWCA paid her to lead a discussion on sex education for Negro adolescent girls and their parents. And she made a hundred dollars for a Model Cities speech and another hundred for a keynote at the State Department of Welfare Conference in Pennsylvania—each payment equivalent to about a thousand dollars today. Bev was also regularly fielding unsolicited job offers. In April 1966 there were two—one from the Graduate School of Social Work at the University of Washington in Seattle and one from NYU's School of Social Work.

Bev was still active with SWCRA, as well. She and David had planned a meeting for the fall called "White Backlash and Black Power," and together they implemented numerous social welfare programs across the city of New York, reaching older populations that were excluded from the work of MFY.

She told Dr. K. about her exciting career developments when she met with him for the first time since before she'd left for Selma.

"It sounds like you have a lot on your plate," Dr. K. said, as Bev settled into her regular spot. She looked around the cramped office and saw that Dr. K. had made some noticeable changes. The walls were painted a pale yellow to replace the dark wood paneling that had been there before. And Dr. K.'s desk was clear and free of the stacks and stacks of files that used to remain there. Bev smiled to herself as she wondered how much input Nancy had had on the redecorating.

"Please tell me that you're making time to take care of yourself," Dr. K. added. "It's been so long since I've seen you; I'm actually more concerned about what's going on in your personal life."

Dr. K. peered at Bev over the top of his glasses like a father checking in on his wayward daughter. And Bev sighed heavily, knowing there was no way to get around this topic of conversation. She gave Dr. K. a brief recap of what had transpired between her and David.

"So you're saying that, before you left for Selma, you were upset because David didn't want to be with you. But when you returned, you decided that you didn't want to be with him, and you were upset because he, then, wanted to be in a relationship with you?" Dr. K.'s face revealed his skepticism.

"First of all, I wasn't *upset*," Bev said impatiently. "And I can't be sure whether he had actually changed his mind about being with me. We never talked about it." As she spoke, she thought back to that day and David's weird behaviors, how he seemed so nervous and antsy. She had replayed the events in her mind so many times, but because it was easier to just forget and move on, she could never be certain how he'd really felt that day.

"What do you mean, you never talked about it?" Dr. K. asked.

"I mean, when he told me why he didn't go to Selma—that he was too afraid—something just clicked inside me. I can't really explain it, but I knew I could probably never really be happy with him. I think I felt that I would always be two steps ahead of him, trying to convince him to keep up with me, and I wouldn't want to be in a relationship like that."

"So you guys just pretended like the conversation never happened—"

"Basically," Bev said, ready to move on. "And it's fine, really. We're still great friends. As a matter of fact, he met someone recently."

"Oh?"

"Her name is Rachel, and she's a second-grade teacher at one of Mobilization for Youth's partner schools. She's beautiful, and I can tell that he really cares about her."

"And how do you feel about that, about his new relationship?"

"Listen, I'm happy for him. Really." Bev's tone was serious. "If we are not meant to be together, I certainly want him to find the person he *is* meant to be with, and she seems like she's the one."

"Okay, I see," Dr. K. replied. "So what about you? Have you been dating?"

Bev told him about Stan Selengut, an architect she'd met the previous summer. He was nice enough, but she felt compelled to break it off with him when it seemed he was content with just casual dating. For Bev, dating was only worth the time if it was moving her closer to getting married.

"Here's the thing, Dr. K.," Bev said. "I am definitely very busy with work and volunteering, so finding a suitable romantic prospect is difficult. But that doesn't mean I'm going to settle. I want nothing more than to build a future that has more in it than work and being a career girl. But I am also happy enough with myself to wait for the right person. I believe that if you want something enough and work for it, you will get it."

Dr. K. smiled at his patient. "Well, Beverly, it looks like

we're out of time. I have a three-thirty appointment that will be here any minute." He stood from his desk and walked around to where she was seated, taking her hand in his. "I want you to know that I am very proud of you," he told her. "You seem so much more mature and confident than you did the last time I saw you — even though you were never really one to lack much confidence!"

Bev laughed. "Thanks for saying that, Dr. K. Selma really did change my life. And thanks for seeing me on such short notice."

"It's no problem, Beverly. And it was certainly good to see you again; just don't wait so long before coming back to see me." Dr. K. hugged her and together they walked out of the office and toward the front of the building.

"We'll see, but I may not be around much longer," Bev said, only half joking. "God may have bigger plans for me than what I can accomplish in New York. And who knows, maybe my husband is back in California."

Dr. K. chuckled. "You're right. There's no telling where you'll end up." He pushed open the door as Bev stepped out to the parking lot. When he noticed the blue Volkswagen parked in front he stopped short. "You bought a car? Beverly, that's excellent!" he exclaimed, clapping his hands together.

"It's nothing," Bev said, laughing at Dr. K.'s excitement over the fact that she was finally driving by herself again after her accident. "I told my mom, and she was really happy for me, too. She asked me what took so long." Bev smiled and shook her head, remembering the conversation. "After Selma, I just figured it was time for me to start making more of my own decisions—in all areas of my life. And as it turns out, that's all Mother ever really wanted."

While Dr. K. watched, Bev walked over to her car and opened the door. And as she tossed her purse onto the passenger seat and sat down, she took inventory of the Volkswagen's interior—the sparkling dashboard that was still free of dust, the factory-installed radio, the wood paneling that shone in the sun's rays filtering through the windows—and marveled at the brand-newness of it all.

Bev placed both hands on the steering wheel and gripped it tightly. She was still getting used to driving again, to finding her place among the other cars on the road and being forced to be cognizant of all the other drivers around her. But there was an overwhelming peace that enveloped her, a knowing that no matter what swirled around outside, within the confines of her Volkswagen, she was the master—and navigator—of her domain.

Then, with the buttery leather pressed firmly between her fingers, Bev steered the car out of Dr. K.'s parking lot, onto Bristol Street and toward her destiny.

ACKNOWLEDGMENTS FROM ANDREA WILLIAMS

To RELIVE THE EXPERIENCES—even through the written word—of the many nameless men and women who worked to make right so many wrongs in American society during the sixties literally brought tears to my eyes. But to share those stories through the lens of someone so unassuming yet fiercely passionate as Bev also gives me tremendous peace and a hope that, where there are still injustices, we can learn from those who came before and unify our efforts in an effective way to bring change.

To my brothers and sisters who set the bar with both focused power and incontestable grace and dignity, there are no words to express my gratitude.

To Karen, Matty, and Meredith, thank you for entrusting me with Bev's story.

And to my husband, Dre, thanks for keeping me on track when visions of white hoods and hanging effigies threatened to pull me under.

ACKNOWLEDGMENTS
FROM
MATTY RICH

IT WOULD BE IMPOSSIBLE to write a book like this—with honesty and multiple perspectives—without the help and assistance of many people who shared stories, events, and personal moments of the life of Beverly Luther-Sims.

My sincere thanks to Andrea Williams for her many hours of creative writing, brainstorming, conference calls, and researching. Andrea's talents were invaluable in the creation of this book.

Thanks to my entertainment-industry friends Gwen Field and Oliver Sims. This book would not have been possible if it wasn't for Oliver's persistence in enlightening me on the story of his stepmother, Beverly Luther-Sims.

Special thanks to Karen Hunter of Karen Hunter Publishing for believing in Bev's story from our first meeting in New York City and helping to make this book come to life. Thank you to Brigitte Smith for all your hard work to bring this book to life at Simon & Schuster.

ACKNOWLEDGMENTS FROM MATTY RICH

Words cannot describe how beyond grateful I am for Noel and Meredith Kopald. Meredith, I am honored to have worked with you to tell the story of your sister, who put her words and skills into action to help African-Americans attain equality during the civil rights era.

I thank my family—my wife, Reid J-Rich, and my mother, Beatrice Richardson, for their love and support.

Lastly, I want to thank the children of Beverly Luther-Sims—Meredith and Martin. I am truly honored to shed light on your mother, her accomplishments, her courageous spirit, and her determination to make America a greater country for all.

As a white woman who worked and marched side by side with African-Americans, Latinos, and Asians during the civil rights movement, Beverly Luther-Sims symbolizes the multiracial and multigenerational crowds whose chants of "Hands up, don't shoot" and "Black lives matter" have united them in protest of the brutal deaths of Michael Brown and Eric Garner, two unarmed black men who were killed by white police officers.

I am so grateful to be a part of Bev's story; for this I am indebted to you all.

ACKNOWLEDGMENTS FROM MEREDITH KOPALD

MY SISTER, BEVERLY LUTHER, was memorable. Her vitality and passion for social justice inspired many and led to meaningful action. *BEV* is the story of her years in New York City, where she founded Social Workers for Civil Rights Action. She joined others to fight injustice, particularly the immediate and deepening denial of voting rights in the South. She traveled to Selma and did her small part in the larger drama of the civil rights movement. I want to acknowledge the hundreds of Bevs, the thousands of people who also went to Selma and experienced remarkable journeys of their own.

I appreciate all those at Simon & Schuster who shepherded my sister's story into print. From the beginning, Karen Hunter boldly embraced the role of a sometimes naïve young white girl in the American narrative of racial and sexual equality. Andrea Williams is central to the book's substance and style. Intuitively sensitive to my sister's character, both Bev and her times found expression in Andrea's informed and felicitous prose. Brigitte Smith's sharp eye for detail was indispensable, as was Elisa Rivlin's advice as they and others guided this book to publication.

There would be no *BEV* without the passion and exemplary persistence of two men: Oliver Sims Jr. and Matty Rich. Oliver's extraordinary effort to bring his stepmother's story to public attention was built on time they spent together and the mutual respect that developed between them. Oliver's friend and filmmaker, Matty Rich, responded to the drama of a young white woman committed to the fight for justice. It was Matty who believed Simon & Schuster would be interested in an ordinary person's work in the cause of civil rights.

My part in telling Bev's story began with her death from lung cancer in December of 1977. She was forty-four. Her children—Martin and Meredith—were six and four years old. It was vital to me that memories of their mother be preserved. I told stories and answered questions throughout their lives, but when Bev's grandchildren began to be born, I sat down and wrote the book upon which *BEV* is based. I hope *BEV* will be meaningful not only to her children but also to readers interested in the history of the civil rights movement, and the role of everyday people committed to making change.